Found Forever

SISTERS AND SERENDIPITY
BOOK TWO

LADY MARIE

Cover design by Lady Marie

Editing by A.K. Edits

Formatting by Lady Marie

Contents

To anyone looking for their forever. Don't worry. We'll find it.

Content Warning

This book contains on-page explicit sexual content, depictions and discussions of partner and parental abandonment, and on-page therapy sessions/interactions.

CHAPTER 1

Lizzie

The gasp that escaped Lizzie was nowhere near as quiet as it should have been, considering she was in her husband's office. Then again, she never could manage to keep her volume to a minimum whenever he dove face-first into her pussy, and that would probably never change. At least, she hoped it wouldn't.

As his tongue flicked across her clit, her thighs clenched, threatening to close, which only caused his grip on her to tighten. "What did I tell you about that? Open up, baby. I'm fucking starving." Alonzo's baritone sent shivers down her spine. She had no choice but to give him exactly what he was asking for.

Putting her full weight on the cherrywood desk beneath her, she spread her legs further apart, bending one so that she was in a more comfortable position, and leaned back on her hands. Lizzie thought about suggesting they clear off his desk altogether so that she could actually sit on it, but Alonzo was clearly pleased with the current angle if the growl he let loose was any indication. Using the fingers on his left hand to keep her lower lips spread, he pressed his tongue flat against her clit, making her hold onto the desk even tighter.

"You know, baby," he said after taking another long lick. God, was he trying to torture her? "I love it when you stop by to bring me my favorite meal." The slurp that followed up his statement made her even wetter. Alonzo always was a bit of a messy eater.

"I wasn't actually supposed to be the meal," she moaned. If it weren't for the distracting feel of his tongue, she might have been able to look across the room where his actual lunch sat abandoned on the couch. The one she was starting to think he'd "forgotten" at home on purpose.

"Oh no, you were definitely supposed to be the meal," he said, confirming her suspicions.

Lizzie couldn't bring herself to be mad at him. Not when he was devouring her pussy like it was the best thing he'd ever tasted. Her hand moved to the back of his head, pulling him in closer. She stopped trying to temper her moans since there really wasn't a need to. The office wasn't completely empty, but Martha —his executive assistant and the person most likely to catch them —wasn't exactly an issue, thanks to the extra hour Alonzo had told her to take for lunch. Thank goodness because otherwise, she'd have to face the older woman knowing she'd heard Lizzie gasping his name as she came all over his face.

Alonzo stared up at her, his chocolate skin providing the perfect complement to her reddish-brown thighs and his salt and pepper goatee glistening with the evidence of all his hard work. Before she could catch her breath, he stood and kissed her. He knew how much being able to taste herself like that turned her on.

When he whispered the words, "Bend over," into her ear, she wasted no time doing as he said. From one moment to the next, her ass was in the air just the way he liked her, and soon he was sliding his long, thick length into her pulsating walls.

"Ahhh, shit," she whimpered as her hands scrambled to get a

grip on whatever they could. Papers. Stapler. Folders. Something, anything for her to hold onto as he stroked into her forcefully over and over again. This never got old. In the four years that they'd been together, she'd never gotten tired of the way his dick seemed to fit her *perfectly*. Never tired of the roll of his hips or the way one of his strong hands always found its way to her short hair while the other gripped her ass.

"What would my employees say if they could see you now? The *illustrious* Mrs. Langston spread open and dripping all over this expensive ass wood?"

She let out a whine at the thought of someone walking in on them, seeing her desperate and moaning. Alonzo lifted one of her legs onto the desk, leaving her even more exposed. She gasped at the feel of the cool air caressing her pussy.

"You look so beautiful taking this dick like the fucking princess you are," he added with another forceful thrust.

"Alonzo, please," she gasped as he fucked into her repeatedly. She wanted to come. She *needed* to come.

"Use your words, baby. Tell me what you're begging for," he grunted as he pulled on her hair. The dull pain only enhanced her pleasure even more.

"Please let me come."

"What was that?" he asked, the bruising grip he had on her hip leaving a stinging sensation.

"Can I come on your dick? *Please*." The words came out as a sob, and the humiliation of it only made her want it more.

The answer she'd been hoping for came almost immediately. "Of course, you can, princess." Alonzo let go of her hip and moved his hand between her legs. As soon as his fingers made contact with her clit, the wave hit her. "Come for me."

Lizzie had no choice but to comply, her sobs filling the room and mixing with the quickening sounds of their bodies meeting. It didn't take long for Alonzo to follow behind, the feel of his cum filling her enough to send aftershocks through her.

"Best. Lunch. Ever," Alonzo said, trying to catch his breath as he slid free. Lizzie could only laugh as she straightened and turned. Their lips connected, the kiss soft and loving until she began to suck on his tongue. She felt him begin to stiffen again, but unfortunately, they didn't have time for a second round.

"Look at you being bad," he groaned, pulling away and putting space between them.

She let out a giggle. "Only for you."

"Yeah, well, you remember that when we get home later." He shot her a wink as he pulled up his pants.

The two of them began to clean up and get themselves together. It would only be a matter of time before someone in the office began heading in their direction, and the impromptu quickie already had Lizzie late for her own job. The post-orgasmic glow she was feeling, though, made it all well worth it.

As she watched her husband straighten his tie and the papers they'd scattered around his desk, a smile broke across her face. Alonzo was everything she could've ever wanted in a partner. Smart, funny, incredibly fucking handsome, skilled in the bedroom (and office), and above all else, kind and thoughtful. If there was anything even close to the perfect man, she knew she had him standing right in front of her. It was wild to think that they were coming up on their third wedding anniversary.

"Why are you looking at me like that?"

She crossed the room and wrapped her arms around his middle. Despite only standing five feet, three inches, she rarely felt small except when she was in his arms. At six feet even, her husband towered over her, and she loved every minute of it. She'd never put much stock into the appeal of height differences, but then again, she hadn't put much thought into a lot of things until the two of them met.

Alonzo pulled her in close, his hands settling on her lower back. "Because I love you." It was the simplest answer she could provide. It was also the one that held the most truth.

"I love you too," he said before placing a few pecks on her lips.

The two separated, and she moved to grab her purse and his actual lunch. "Here. As delicious as my pussy might be, it's not as nutritious as this."

"So you think," he said, a mischievous grin playing on his lips.

Lizzie rolled her eyes and handed him the meal in question. She pulled her lower lip between her teeth. "Can you pick up Christian today? I'm going to be a little later getting off than I initially thought. And not just because of this distraction."

"Of course. How about he and I grab dinner on the way home, too? That way, you won't have to worry about anything but finishing up with your clients and making your way home to us."

"That would be amazing." She blew him a kiss and headed toward the door. "You treat me like such a queen," she said, looking back at him.

"Because that's exactly what you are."

CHAPTER 2

Alonzo

"You been in here fucking, haven't you?"

Alonzo didn't even bother looking up from his desk. He knew the other man was just trying to get a rise out of him the only way someone he called his business partner and best friend could. "Don't you have anything better to do than come in here on your usual bullshit?"

"According to my schedule, I'm actually right on time with my usual bullshit." Oliver Hayes took a seat in front of Alonzo's desk, and Lonzo knew without looking that his signature smirk adorned his face.

"You also didn't deny my accusation, so you pretty much just told on yourself."

"Is that what you think?" Alonzo asked, his eyes finally leaving the stack of papers in front of him with a smirk of his own.

"It's what I know. Especially since a few little birdies around here mentioned seeing the Missus leaving about an hour ago as they were coming back from a long lunch. One that I hear you encouraged—wait, no, *insisted* on."

"Lizzie just stopped by to drop off my lunch. I was in such a rush this morning that I left it on the counter."

"Mhmm, and I'm sure that mistake happened completely by accident," Oliver responded skeptically.

"Of course," Alonzo answered with a wolfish grin.

Oliver just shook his head as he chuckled knowingly. The insatiable appetite that Alonzo had for his wife wasn't anything new. "Anyway, since I know you have no real interest in telling me exactly how you spent your lunch hour, and I'm personally not all that interested in hearing the details, let's move on to why I'm really here. I was wondering if you had a chance to take a look at my recommendations for the Aldridge account."

"I did," Alonzo said, finally giving the other man his full attention. He leaned back in his chair, stroking his recently trimmed beard.

"And?"

"And…while I think that he could stand to take an extra risk or two, your assessment is pretty spot on. Expanding his portfolio into real estate is the most practical move, especially since he's looking for longevity in his returns. Besides, I'm all for assisting Black men in creating generational wealth, and we both know that real estate is one of the best ways to achieve that."

When Alonzo and Oliver decided to take on the task of starting their own financial consulting firm, they both agreed to prioritize working with a clientele that was predominantly Black and of color. Too often, those communities were ignored, something they'd witnessed time and time again at their previous company. While making money was certainly never a bad thing, they also wanted to be able to pass on their expertise and knowledge to people within their own community. Alonzo had seen firsthand how often his friends and family growing up were left in the dark or taken advantage of when trying to make financial decisions. It was important to him to do what he could to empower others and combat inequality. That was why, in addition to taking on various high-profile paying clients, he and Oliver both did pro bono work in the form of financial literacy classes in various settings, set aside a weekend each month dedicated to financial advising to those unable to afford it, and assisted local small businesses in networking and connecting with the right resources. They also made sure that each consultant who joined their firm was able to dedicate a certain number of hours each month to the pro bono project of their choice. Wealth and knowledge meant nothing if you couldn't help uplift those around you. It was actually during one of those financial literacy classes that Alonzo met Lizzie.

She'd been toying with the idea of starting her own business with a few women who were in cosmetology school with her but realized she had no idea what that entailed. She'd also shared with the class her desire to learn how to be more financially independent in a way that didn't leave her struggling every month and left room for indulgences every now and again. While Lizzie hadn't been the only person who'd voiced that sentiment, the way her nose had bunched up while mentioning having no clue where her money was going every month had been one of the cutest things he'd ever seen. He still had that exact thought whenever the same look appeared on her face.

"Great," Oliver said, pulling Alonzo from his thoughts. "I have a briefing scheduled with him on Monday, so I'll finalize a few things, and then we'll be ready to go."

Alonzo nodded, knowing his friend had everything perfectly in hand. There was a reason he trusted Oliver with both his business and his life. He hadn't found a better friend since the two met around twenty-three years ago during their sophomore year at Oakwood University. Even then, with all his bravado and jokes, it wasn't hard to tell that Oliver was the type of man who could always be depended on.

When Alonzo had come to him about leaving their previous job, Oliver's response hadn't been to ask him a slew of questions. Instead, he only asked one: "What the hell took you so long?"

It'd been hard work, and in a lot of ways, the two men had been forced to start from the ground up, but they'd managed to create something that they could both be proud of. Whatever bridges may have been burned on their departure, whatever slights the partners had claimed to feel, hadn't stopped them from prospering. Of course, it helped that a few of their clients also believed in what they were looking to create and vowed to move their accounts wherever the two men landed.

"So, now that that's out of the way, any plans tonight? I was thinking of heading down to Titan for a bit." The mention of their favorite cigar lounge, which they'd been frequenting at least once a week for the last five years, was enticing, to say the least. Unfortunately, Alonzo already had a commitment for the night.

"Tempting," he sighed, "but I told Lizzie I'd pick Christian up from school and take care of dinner tonight since she'll be at the shop a little late."

"Okay, no problem. How about tomorrow night? I think D'Angelo mentioned something about a new shipment of bourbon coming in that he wanted us to taste test before adding it to the menu."

"No can do. That's Lizzie's night with her sisters, which means that Christian and I will be at home scarfing down pizza and wings while he beats my ass in every game imaginable." He chuckled at the thought, knowing that his stepson had already most likely picked out at least four video games for them to play. Probably a couple of board games, too. "And I think Reggie mentioned something about stopping by."

Oliver was already familiar with his sister-in-law's boyfriend since the three of them had been involved in their fair share of business deals long before Reggie had been introduced to Makayla.

"Damn, Reggie got the invite but not me? That's cold-blooded, bruh."

"You are more than welcome to come, and you already know that. Matter of fact, we'll let you treat. Pizza and wings on you."

"You lucky I love my nephew the way I do," Oliver said.

The claim he put on Christian was another thing Alonzo appreciated about his friend. When Lizzie came into his life and made it clear that she and her son were a package deal, Oliver didn't even think twice about accepting the little boy as his own family, much like Alonzo. The two of them spent countless hours taking the youngblood out to ball games, arcades, guys' weekends, and anything else they could think of.

"Speaking of Reggie, don't think I've forgotten about the fact you used him to ruin my chances with Makayla. I mean, if you didn't want me to be your brother-in-law, that's all you had to say."

"Nigga, please! How many times do I have to tell you you didn't stand a chance?" Alonzo responded with full-bodied laughter.

"Only because you wouldn't help a brother out!"

Over the last few years, Oliver had flirted with Makayla in public whenever their paths crossed while asking Alonzo to put in a good word for him in private. Each and every time, he told his friend the same thing: Hell. No. Truth be told, Makayla would probably chew his ass up and spit him out, but more than that, he knew that Oliver, no matter how much he loved his friend, was just not what the woman needed.

"Sorry, old man, but her and Reggie? That shit was written in the stars."

Kissing his teeth, Oliver stood and shook his head. "Whatever, man. I'm officially clearing my schedule for tomorrow night. Prepare to get your ass beat in Chutes and Ladders or whatever the kids are playing these days."

Alonzo just laughed as his friend exited the room and closed the door behind him. Looking from the papers in front of him to his computer, he decided it was time to get back to business. If there was any hope of getting out of there in time to pick up Christian from school, he really needed to buckle down and get some work done. No more distractions allowed for the rest of the day.

CHAPTER 3

Lizzie

"**B**itch, not you walking in here with the type of glow that only a quickie can provide." Of course, Raven, Lizzie's best friend and business partner, would be the one to put her on blast as soon as she walked into their shop, Vivid Beauty Bar.

"I have no idea what you're talking about," Lizzie responded, trying to keep the look on her face as innocent as possible as she headed over to her station.

"Lying is not your lane, honey. Stick to the rivers and the lakes that you're used to," her bestie cackled.

"Raven's right, babe," added Peyton, one of their other stylists. "You definitely have that fresh orgasmic glow going on. And considering you're twenty minutes late and you have a husband who worships the ground you walk on, we can only come to one conclusion."

"You got some cutty this morning!" multiple voices rang out, followed by laughter.

"Okay, first of all, every time y'all come to work, *ATL* does not need to be in rotation." Lizzie couldn't help but laugh along with them. "Second, act like y'all have some home training. I know you see all these clients up in here." She gestured around to each station, most of which were occupied.

"Oh, please, we've all been coming here long enough to know how this thing goes. Don't try to act all bougie now just because you don't wanna clue us in on your afternoon delight," Nadine, one of her regulars, said.

Lizzie gave her a pointed look as she grabbed her apron. "You might want to pipe down before you end up looking like Cruella de Vil up in here. Don't forget who's got the hair dye."

"Girl, you better not! You know I have a hot date tonight!" She paused. "Actually, he does have all those damn animals, so he might be into the whole Disney look. It could work in my favor. You never know."

"Girl, go sit your wild ass at my station!"

"I'm going, I'm going..."

This was one of the things that Lizzie loved about her job. Not only did it allow her the opportunity to express her creativity, but it also helped her develop close relationships. Most of her regular clients felt more like friends than anything. This was supposed to be a place where people could come to relax, do some self-care, or reinvent themselves. They offered a little bit of everything: various types of natural and relaxed haircare, loc and braid along with wig and weave services, and nail treatments. This shop was her happy place, and she wanted it to be that way for others too.

"Anyway, without oversharing, did you go see that fine ass husband of yours or not?" Peyton asked as he expertly worked on his client's knotless undercolor braids. He was one of the best braiders she'd ever encountered, and both she and Raven had been ecstatic when he expressed interest in leaving his previous shop and coming to work with them.

"I did. He forgot his lunch at home, so I stopped over to drop it off while I was running errands."

"Mhmm, and I'm sure you gave him a bit of dessert while you were there," he teased. "I ain't mad at you. If I had me a nigga like that on the line, I too would be doing drop-ins so he could pop it in." That one got shrieks of laughter from everyone in the shop, including Lizzie. Peyton was a hot ass mess. She knew they were just teasing, but she also couldn't deny just how right they all were. Nothing brightened up her day more than seeing her husband, except maybe spending time with her six-year-old son Christian. Both of them were truly the lights of her life. And so, she let her co-workers clown her all they wanted. There was no shame in her game. Sometimes a pop-in was exactly what the stylist ordered.

———

After several hours of cuts, dyes, and masterfully laying edges, Lizzie was ready to head home. She was exhausted and wanted nothing more than to get home and soak in her oversized bathtub. She silently thanked the Lord for Alonzo's idea that he take care of dinner because she was too tired to make any stops after closing up.

"You ready to head out?" Raven asked her as she came from doing inventory in the backroom.

"Absolutely," Lizzie said, stifling a yawn. Just as she turned off her station light and grabbed her purse, her cell phone started going off. Seeing a number she didn't recognize, she scrunched up her face. Maybe it was a new client. Even though she had a separate business line, sometimes referrals came through on her personal number. She thought about letting it go to voicemail but decided to pick up at the last minute.

"Hello?" she said, only to be met with dead air. "Hello?" she said again. There was nothing but silence, so she hung up.

Wrong number, I guess.

Heading toward the door, she started to say something to

Raven, but her phone rang again, the same number coming across her screen.

"Hello?" Silence. *Again.* Now she was getting irritated. "Listen, I don't appreciate you wasting my time. Is anyone there?" The last thing she wanted to do was be rude to a potential client, but she was too tired to be dealing with bullshit tonight.

"Who was that?" Raven asked as Lizzie ended the call.

"Girl, I have no clue." As soon as the words left her mouth, her phone began going off for the third time. This time she picked up without even taking a look at the screen.

"Listen, play on my phone one more time and—"

"Damn, girl! All of that energy, though?" came a familiar voice.

"Morgan?" Lizzie said, pulling the phone away from her ear. Sure enough, her close friend's picture was staring back at her on the screen. "Girl, did you just call me from a different number?"

"Umm…no, why?"

"Someone called me a couple times back-to-back, but when I answered, it was literally dead silent on the other end. Fucking weird."

"Yeah," Morgan answered, "people are weird as hell." Lizzie raised an eyebrow because something about the other woman's tone sounded a little off. Maybe she was just imagining things.

"So, what's up?" She finally followed Raven out of the door, not wanting to hold her friend up anymore. She gave her a silent goodbye before heading to her own car.

"Umm…" The silence that followed was so prominent that Lizzie had to pull her phone away from her ear again to make sure they hadn't gotten disconnected.

"Hello?"

"Yeah, umm…I just wanted to make sure you were still bringing dessert to the book club meeting on Monday."

Oookay. "Uhh, yeah. I mean, I'm always on dessert duty, so that was the plan."

Morgan gave a weak laugh. "I don't know, girl. You might have wanted to switch things up a bit or something. Just had to check. Anyway, I know you're probably headed home, so I'll just see you in a few days."

"Okay. See you then."

Lizzie hung up and shook her head. She didn't know what was going on but decided to just shake it off. Home was calling her name, and she was ready to answer.

CHAPTER 4

Lizzie

"Oh! I forgot to tell y'all. Lonzo and I finally decided on what to do for our anniversary!" Even though she was in the living room, Lizzie knew that both of her older sisters could hear her.

It was their monthly 'For Sissas Only' night. Once a month, usually on a Friday, the trio put aside everything in the outside world, from work to other family to romantic partners, and spent time together, just the three of them. Depending on how they felt, they would go all out with the planning and activities or decide to keep it lowkey with a movie or game night. It didn't really matter what they did as long as they did it together. Tonight's activity of choice was wine and movies at Makayla's house, a combination that could never go wrong.

It was still a fairly new concept for them, something they'd instituted after Makayla and Kendall had nearly come to blows during a group spa day right before their mother's wedding. That was the day that they found out that not only was Makayla dealing with some heavy insecurities regarding her love life (partly due to her family's actions and judgments), but Kendall was going through her own marital drama with her husband. It became pretty clear that while the sisters certainly loved one another, they hadn't been connected in a very long time. They all came to the conclusion that they needed to put more effort into rebuilding their relationship. Thus, 'For Sissas Only' was born.

"I'm surprised he's not just whisking you away for some extremely romantic vacation," Kendall said as she walked into the room, set two bottles of wine on the coffee table, and made herself comfortable in Makayla's new egg chair.

"That's not completely off the table. At least, I don't think it is. We've been talking about taking a vacation, possibly of the couples variety." She threw a mischievous look toward both her sisters but didn't go any further since Kendall looked like she was jumping out of her skin at the suggestion. "Y'all know how much I love country music and whiskey, right? So, we've decided to have our own lil' version of a honky-tonk!"

Lizzie's excitement was evident, especially since she threw a little twang in there for good measure, but neither Kendall nor Makayla, who had just walked into the room with the sushi, were matching her energy.

"Ummm, you did hear me, right? We're having a good ole fashioned honky-tonk!" she repeated just in case they hadn't understood.

"Yeah, we heard. I'm just trying to figure out what about our Black ass family says 'honky-tonk' to you," said Kendall.

"Right. Like, you do realize that we're not a bunch of white folk, right?" Makayla added.

Lizzie kissed her teeth. "First of all, country music belonged to Black people first, okay, and we are well on our way to taking it back." While she loved Reba and Dolly just as much as any country music fan, Lizzie was even more excited to know that there were a lot more Black faces getting acknowledgment in the country scene these days. "Second, it'll be fun! We're going to rent out this new spot downtown that opened up a few weeks ago. The owner worked with Lonzo's company and told him they're more than happy to rent the space out to us for a discounted price. Seeing it during the grand opening is what gave me the idea in the first place. It's such a chill place, and their barbeque is fucking bomb! Plus, it's Black-owned."

Both of her sisters looked skeptical, which only made her roll her eyes. Sad how she was the only one in the family who had any real musical taste. "Anyway, both of you just better start looking for cute cowboy hat and boot combos. No half-assing it." She gave each of them a pointed look. "Attendance is mandatory, so don't even think about skipping out. Besides, I don't know why y'all are acting like this is a shock. Our first dance was literally to Rascal Flatts' version of 'Bless the Broken Road.'" Not only had the song fit their love story, but it was one of her absolute favorites.

"Why does everything in this family have to be a damn production?" Makayla teased as she took her seat on the couch. "Like nothing can ever just be a simple dinner."

"One, because we love having a good time, and two, I know you're not complaining considering the fact that the last 'production' this family had resulted in you being booed up with that very fine ass specimen you call your man." Lizzie tossed popcorn at the other woman to aid in her teasing.

It was hilarious to think that just a few months ago, Makayla had managed to convince Reggie to pretend to be her boyfriend and date to their mother's wedding. He must've already been head over heels for her, considering he agreed and played the role well. They definitely had Lizzie fooled, and she was the one who'd set them up in the first place. Not only had they managed to pull the whole thing off, but they'd also fallen in love in the process. The two of them were made for each other, and she'd honestly never seen her big sister happier.

"He *is* fine, isn't he?" The look on Makayla's face said that she was thinking about something extremely specific. Knowing her, it was probably something nasty.

"Okay, enough of that! I came here for sister time, not to watch M&M rehash some lil' nasty moment she and Reggie had recently." Kendall's words were accompanied by an eye roll and a smile, showing just how far they'd come. If this had been a few months ago, there definitely would have been a bite to her words.

"I second that," Lizzie said, following it up with a fake gag.

Makayla kissed her teeth. "Hating is such a disease. Get well soon, bitches." As soon as the words left her mouth, Lizzie could see that she was having a momentary look of panic, one that she was sure was reflected in her own eyes as her gaze flitted over to Kendall.

Luckily, the oldest of the sisters seemed to be taking the comment in stride. "Well, I'll be sure to make a doctor's appointment. In the meantime, keep a lid on all that freaky shit." The laugh that followed confirmed that there was no malice behind them, though there did seem to be a hint of sadness in her eyes.

Figuring it was best to take at least some of the heat off of her sister, Lizzie said, "Back to the situation at hand. I'm serious, y'all. I know three years isn't exactly a milestone year, but I would really love it if everyone could celebrate with us."

"We know, we know. Don't worry, Lizzie. We'll all be there," Makayla said, sending a smile her way.

Of course, the question of whether or not that meant that Kendall's husband Greg would be there was a tiny elephant in the room, but for now, she'd leave it alone. They'd have to cross the bridge soon, but not tonight.

"Now that my announcement is out of the way, pass me the sushi. I'm starving."

The next ninety minutes passed in a blur of wine, sashimi, shrimp tempura rolls, and one of their favorite girls' trip comedies. By the time the movie ended, all three of them were crying with laughter. These were the moments that Lizzie cherished. She loved spending time with Christian and Alonzo, but something about being with her sisters really made her feel at peace.

Kendall's clap drew her attention. "Okay, ten-minute potty break, and then ice cream before movie two," she said, hopping up from her seat.

"Aye, aye, captain." Before Lizzie could make a move, her phone rang. Grabbing it just in case it was Alonzo calling about Christian, she gave the screen a confused look when she saw it was the same number that had called her the day before. Considering whoever it was had been playing on her phone enough, she chose to send them straight to voicemail.

After taking care of her personal business in the guest bathroom and grabbing the ice cream out of the freezer, she reclaimed her seat on the couch. Neither of her sisters was back yet, and if she had to guess, they were both probably taking the little bit of time they had left to check in at home. Greg had taken the kids to his mom's house, and Reggie was having game night with Alonzo, Christian, and Oliver.

While she waited for them to come back, she noticed that whoever had called her decided to leave a message. "I swear to God if this is just them breathing on the phone again..." she grumbled as she pressed play. As soon as she heard the voice behind the number, she found herself wishing it'd actually been silence on the other end.

"What's up, Bug? Shit, I, uh...I hope this is your number, and Morgan didn't just give me a random to shut me up. If this ain't Lizette Michaels, feel free to delete this message. If it is Lizzie, well, I hope you ain't already decided to hang up anyway. This is, umm...well, if you haven't figured it out yet, it's King. I know it's been a minute, but...well, I was hoping we could catch up. Shit, I..."

There was a pause before his next words.

"Just hit me up, Bug. I really wanna see you."

Lizzie was left speechless. She couldn't be sure how long she sat there, staring at her phone, but it was long enough for both of her sisters to come back and get settled in their places.

"Alright, who's ready for—" Whatever Makayla had been about to say died on her lips when she saw Lizzie's face.

"What's wrong, babe??" she asked, scooting closer to her. It wasn't until Makayla's thumb swiped at her cheek that Lizzie even realized she'd started crying. God, how pathetic was that? One little message, and suddenly she turned into a whole mess.

"Is it Christian?" Kendall asked, her voice full of concern.

"Yes." Lizzie shook her head quickly before either one of them could panic. "I mean no. I mean…shit." She took a few deep breaths hoping they would help her calm down and collect her thoughts. "Christian is fine, but…" No matter how much she tried to form the words, they just wouldn't come. So, she did the next best thing: played them the message. The other two women were just as speechless when it was all said and done. Well, almost.

"Bitch, was that your baby daddy?!" Makayla exclaimed.

"Yep," Lizzie choked out. "It sure was."

CHAPTER 5

Alonzo

Something wasn't right. Alonzo noticed it the moment that Lizzie walked through the door that morning. The bubbly woman who'd gone to spend the night with her sisters was not the one avoiding his gaze across the kitchen island. The way that she was worrying the inside of her top lip let him know that something was weighing heavily on her mind.

They'd been sitting in silence for almost ten minutes. Since it was clear she wasn't going to break it first, Alonzo decided to try his luck. "You wanna tell me what's wrong, or would you rather chew that lip of yours raw?" he asked as he leaned across the top of the island. His hand moved to cover hers, and it struck him, as it always did, just how small they were in comparison to his.

Her eyes fluttered up to meet his before they quickly looked in another direction. "Something happened last night. Or rather, someone happened last night, and I don't..." Lizzie took a breath and tried to steady her words. "I don't want to hide this from you."

Alonzo tried his best not to let her words rattle him. They'd always agreed to be open and honest with each other no matter what. It was decided early on that having an open line of communication was the best thing they could do for their relationship. Beyond that, Lizzie always talked about how much she appreciated him being such a steady presence for her. In situations where she might be prone to panic or her nerves tended to get the best of her, he always managed to help her navigate and stay calm. She didn't expect him to be perfect and knew that there were things that could knock him off guard as well, but when he could help it, he worked hard to keep a level head. The last thing he wanted was to add to her panic about whatever this was. So, even though her words sent a bolt of fear through him, he focused on what he could control: his reaction.

"I appreciate that, sweetheart. Whatever it is, though, we'll get through it like we always do. Together." He placed what he hoped was a reassuring kiss along her knuckles. She still looked unsure, but that was fine. He knew how to be patient. If she decided that she didn't want to talk about whatever it was right now, then he'd wait until she was ready.

It took a bit longer before she said anything else, but when she did, he had to work a lot harder to hold his composure. "I got a phone call last night…from King."

King. King *fucking* Holden. Alonzo had to admit the man clearly had a set of balls on him. Or maybe just no sense of self-preservation. Maybe he still hadn't learned how to make smart decisions. Alonzo wouldn't put it past him. He wasn't sure which one would account for disappearing on your girlfriend less than forty-eight hours after she gives birth to your newborn and then not reaching out to either of them more than twice for the next six years. The goddamn audacity was astounding. He'd never understand how a person could abandon someone they claimed to love.

Alonzo must've taken longer than he thought to process what she'd said because when Lizzie started speaking again, her words came out in a rush. "Remember those phone calls I told you about the other day when I came home? Well, turns out they were from King. He called me again from the same number last night. I didn't answer it because I figured whoever it was was just playing on my phone again, but he left a message this time." He watched as Lizzie started to pick at her nails. Her eyes moved toward the ceiling, and he could see that she was trying not to cry, which only made Alonzo even more upset. Not with Lizzie, of course, but with King. With him and how easily he'd already put Lizzie on edge.

He walked around the island, pulled her out of her seat, and pulled her body into his. "Hey, it's fine, sweetheart. I'm fine, you're fine, Christian is fine." His fingers rubbed circles at the back of her neck. That always seemed to calm her down a bit. He felt her breathing begin to even out, one deep breath after the other.

She finally released a groan. "How does he do this? How does he get me this flustered this quickly with nothing but a damn voicemail?"

"Everyone has someone who does exceptionally well when it comes to getting under their skin. Unfortunately, King happens to be that person for you."

"Yeah, but after almost seven years, babe? All that time, and now suddenly, he's blowing up my line trying to get a hold of me. I swear, he's like a fucking infestation."

Alonzo grunted, fully agreeing with her. "What did the message say?" he asked, pulling away just enough to see her face.

Lizzie took a step out of his arms and grabbed her phone off the island. After unlocking it and navigating through a few screens, she brought up the voicemail. Soon, what Alonzo could only assume was King's voice filled the kitchen, and he had to fight to keep his temper under control. Six years later and he couldn't be bothered to ask how his son was doing or ask to see him. No, his main concern was seeing Lizzie.

"Unclench, babe," Lizzie said, clearly noticing how tense he'd gotten. Her fingers ghosted over his jaw, and it had the desired effect almost immediately. He willed himself to relax so that at the very least, he wouldn't be in danger of cracking a tooth.

He went to say something and then stopped as a thought occurred to him. "He said something about Morgan giving him your number. She didn't mention anything or give you some sort of heads up?"

He watched as his wife's face went from sadness to straight irritation. "Hell no! And trust me when I say she's getting a damn earful about it, too. Especially since I told her about the weird phone calls. I thought she acted strange when I brought them up, but I just brushed it off, thinking I was being weird." She grumbled something else that he didn't completely catch, but he was pretty sure the words 'ass' and 'whooping' were in there somewhere.

Alonzo gave her a soft smile. "Go easy on her, babe. She didn't exactly get to choose her family, and honestly, I wouldn't be surprised if he caught her just as off guard as he caught you with his phone calls."

She kissed her teeth. "Knowing King, you're probably right."

His eyes drifted toward the phone before landing back on her. "So, what do you want to do?" he asked, skating right to the point. Knowing Lizzie the way he did, Alonzo knew that part of the reason she was so upset was because she was struggling to figure out what to do next.

"Well, first and foremost, I want to call Dr. Brunson and move up my therapy session because I feel extremely close to being out of control in a way that I haven't felt in a very long time. I definitely need help processing all of this."

"Okay, so let's make sure you do that as soon as possible, then. I'm sure she can fit you in before the week is out."

"Already taken care of. I left a message with her assistant to see if she had any last-minute openings," she said, clearly proud that she was already one step ahead of her husband.

Alonzo couldn't help the sense of pride that flowed through him in that moment. Her self-awareness was one of his favorite things about her. She was more in tune with her needs than almost anyone else he knew. He knew that she hadn't gotten there overnight and that her work in therapy before they'd met and after they'd gotten together played a role, but considering how therapy was seen in the Black community in general, he loved the fact that she did what she needed to keep herself healthy. Even though he was several years her senior, he wouldn't hesitate to admit that when it came to certain areas, Lizzie was certainly the more mature of the two.

He gave her a smile. "Okay, so that's checked off the list. What's second?"

"Second…I want to know what you think I should do." The confidence that had been in her tone just a few seconds ago disappeared, replaced by uncertainty.

He took a moment before answering. Alonzo had never been one to tell Lizzie, or anyone else, for that matter, what they should do unless it was in a professional manner with a client. As much as he wanted to tell her to ignore the bastard and go on acting as if he didn't exist, he knew he had no right to ask that of her.

"Unfortunately, sweetheart, I don't think I can tell you what to do here."

"Seriously? You're never bossy when I need you to be," she huffed. He couldn't help but laugh at that.

"I think we both know that I'm the boss at exactly the right times." He lifted an eyebrow and gave her a knowing look.

His statement lightened the mood just enough that he saw more tension leave her shoulders. "Okay, you're right," she said, rolling her eyes, though a smile appeared on her face. "I just…I don't know what to do about this."

Alonzo pulled her back to him, hands moving to frame her

face. "And that's okay. You don't have to have all the answers right now. Put a pin in it and come back to it later."

"But—" she started before he stopped her with a kiss. It was soft, his lips slanting over hers, and ended in the span of a few breaths.

"But nothing. If you decide you want to meet up to hear him out, I'll support you. If you decide you want to say screw him and ignore the message, I'll support that too. Either way, nothing has to be decided right at this moment, so don't stress yourself out about it."

"So, what do you suggest I do instead?"

"Well," he said, placing another kiss on her lips, this one a little longer than the last, "I happen to know for a fact that your two favorite guys missed you while you were gone." Alonzo was happy to see a smile appear on her lips. "And while I love having you all to myself, I'm thinking you should go and wake up Christian so that I can take you both out for brunch. Get this Saturday back on track."

This time, her smile spread from ear to ear. "I think I can definitely do that."

CHAPTER 6

Lizzie

Lizzie did not expect the first words out of her mouth as she entered Morgan's living room to be, "I just need to know if you want me to whoop your ass now or if you'd prefer I wait until *after* you've finished going over this month's book," but somehow, that's exactly what came out. Clearly, her emotions had gotten the best of her.

She'd been contemplating what exactly she wanted to say to her friend for the entire weekend. She'd been so caught off guard by King mentioning Morgan in the message, and the more she thought about it, the more she'd wanted to call her and curse her out. Alonzo had convinced her during their day out with Christian that it would be better for her to take some time and really think on what she was feeling and what she wanted to say. The thought was that taking that time before they saw each other face-to-face would help her be a bit more rational and understanding. That obviously went out the window.

The last thing she wanted to do was go off in front of one of her closest friends, especially in front of their monthly book club. She certainly didn't want to put Morgan in the middle of whatever King was trying to get going. Then again, as his cousin, she was already in the middle if you really thought about it. Morgan was the only person from her past with King that Lizzie still kept in touch with. After King introduced them, they had become casual friends. Once he disappeared, Morgan made it a point to step up and not only be a great friend to Lizzie but family to both her and Christian.

In many ways, Morgan was the only family member he ever really had since King's parents passed away when he was in middle school and his grandparents long before that. After their death, he moved in with Morgan and her parents. According to King, the two had already been practically inseparable, more like siblings than cousins. Years later, after Lizzie met him, Morgan confided in her that while she loved King like a brother, she never imagined that would also include cleaning up after him on a regular basis. It seemed as though she was still sitting in that same role.

All five other women in the room, including Morgan and Raven, looked shocked by Lizzie's outburst. "Well damn, girl, the book was bad, but it certainly wasn't that bad," Morgan said with a laugh, the other ladies joining in.

"I'm not talking about the damn book!" she said with a frustrated growl, even though, yeah, the book Morgan had picked for the month hadn't exactly been the best read. "I'm talking about King showing up in my fucking life again with his bullshit without any sort of warning from you, my *friend*."

That stopped everyone in their tracks. Considering Raven was Lizzie's best friend, and the other three women were close friends with Morgan, everyone knew the significance of that name. "Okay, everyone, nothing to see here!" Raven said, hopping out of her seat. She quickly ushered everyone else toward the kitchen to give the two women some privacy.

"King?" Morgan whispered, still seemingly shocked.

"Yep. You know, your favorite brother-cousin? The one who

got me pregnant and disappeared into the sunset all by himself
six years ago? Apparently, he's decided to reappear and give me a
call since he managed to get my number—from *you*, I might
add."

The shock left Morgan's face, and what replaced it seemed to
be something akin to guilt. "Shit."

"Yeah, shit is right." Lizzie took a seat across from her, trying
hard to sort through her emotions. She was pissed off, that was
for damn sure. On top of that, she was frustrated with the situation, with her reaction, and with Morgan's actions. Confusion
and hurt were in there somewhere as well. Morgan may not have
deserved the brunt of her outburst, but as far as Lizzie was
concerned, she'd definitely earned some of it. The other woman
may be King's family, but wasn't that what she had been to
Morgan as well for all these years?

"Just be honest with me, Morgan. No bullshit. Is King telling
the truth? Did you give him my number? Did you know he was
back in town?"

After a few moments of silence, she nodded her head. "Yeah.
Yeah, I gave him your number." Lizzie immediately kissed her
teeth, feeling her temper rise again. "But I swear I didn't know he
was in town!"

"Why would you give him my number in the first place?"

"Because he's Christian's father! He deserves to be able to
contact you and Christian, and it's not fair that he doesn't have a
way to do that."

"Absolutely not," Lizzie snapped. "First of all, let's not act
like I changed my number to keep Christian away from King. I
even tried to reach out to him to give him the number when I
first changed it years ago, and you know that! He was the one
who was unreachable." She was not about to let that narrative fly.
If he was so worried about keeping up with his child, he would
have answered one of the dozens of times she'd called him the
first few years of Christian's life or, at the very least, had the

decency not to change his number so often that she finally stopped trying. "Second, Christian has a father, and his name certainly isn't King. King is the name of his sperm donor. Alonzo Langston is his father, point blank, period. And third, King doesn't deserve a damn thing from me."

Morgan at least had the decency to look ashamed of her comments. "Okay, that's fair. I'm sorry. I know King hasn't exactly been a father or a good person since Christian was born." That was an understatement. Truth be told, King was barely a decent person before he left. "But he is my cousin, babe. My blood. He's made some shitty choices, for sure, but he's really changed this time. Don't you think he should have the opportunity to show you that? To see what an amazing kid he missed out on?"

"Honestly? No." That was Lizzie's immediate answer, but after a few seconds, she groaned. "Maybe? Honestly, I don't know, okay." She leaned back against the chair and closed her eyes. "What I do know is that I don't need him coming in here up to his old tricks. I don't need him screwing with Christian's emotions. My baby does not deserve that kind of pain in his life. And he for sure doesn't need you making life-altering decisions for him or this family, Morgan. It's over the line, and you know it on multiple levels. Don't forget, I'm not the only one that your cousin has shitted on over the years." Lizzie gave her friend a pointed look.

"You're right, and I'm sorry," she responded, sounding properly chastised. "I just… I want better for King, you know? That boy has always been my weakness. He fucks up, and I come in and save the day. That's always been our dynamic."

"Yeah, well, he's not a little boy anymore, Morgan. He's a grown man, so how about we try letting him save the day on his own from now on? And next time, ask before you decide to do a familial good deed. Your heart may have been in the right place, but you absolutely went about it the wrong way."

"Agreed," Morgan said, standing. Lizzie followed suit, allowing the other woman to pull her into a hug.

Despite how upset she may have been initially, Lizzie knew that Morgan didn't mean any harm. She loved Christian just as much as anyone. Even still, the truth was everywhere King went, he caused chaos. After all, chaos was what the man did best.

CHAPTER 7

Alonzo

Alonzo hadn't stopped laughing since Lizzie'd walked through the door and told him what happened at her book club. When she'd left the house, she'd been calm and ready to talk to her friend to try and get some answers. At some point, that had gone out the window, and she'd managed to get herself riled up enough to walk in threatening the other woman in front of everyone. He just couldn't manage to contain his chuckles whenever the mental image of his wife barging into Morgan's house, face scrunched and steam probably coming out of her ears, reappeared.

"Lonzo, it's not funny," Lizzie groaned as she tied her scarf around her head, staring at him through the mirror.

"It's a little funny." She shot him a look, and he threw his hands up in surrender. "Okay, okay, I'm sorry. You're right, it's not funny. I just...you really walked in there and told Morgan you were going to beat her ass?" Alonzo came up behind her and wrapped his arms around her waist, chin nestling itself on top of her head as she braced her hands on the counter of the his-and-her bathroom sink.

"I don't know! I was just so damn mad, and it got worse once I actually saw her face." She shook her head. "And between me and you, I know I could've taken her."

"You damn right," he said, a smirk on his face as he kissed the top of her head. "But I'm glad you didn't have to." Despite how upset the situation made her, and him for that matter, Alonzo knew that fighting with Morgan was the last thing that Lizzie wanted to do, no matter how mad she may have been. It might have felt satisfying in the moment, but when it was all said and done, it would have only ended with her being hurt.

"Want me to run you a bubble bath?" he asked, his eyes staring into hers through the reflection.

A small smile found its way to her lips. "Yes, please."

Giving her waist a squeeze, he turned toward their oversized soaking tub and ran the hot water, adding her favorite essential oils, bath salts, and bubbles just the way she liked. It didn't take long for him to deem the water perfect, and he was getting ready to tell Lizzie just that when he turned around and noticed her watching him intently as she dropped her silk floral robe to the floor. As his eyes raked over her, he felt his dick stiffen. Fuck, he loved his wife's body. The way her breasts were just more than a perfect handful, how her hips flared out from her waist, those dimples in her dark thighs that she hated but he was absolutely obsessed with because they matched the one in her left cheek. She was nothing less than a masterpiece.

"You're staring."

He finally brought his eyes up and found her smirking, that left dimple that he loved so much staring back at him. "I'm pretty sure that's exactly what you wanted, princess."

"Maybe," she said, hips swaying as she made her way to the tub. The sound of his hand colliding with her ass echoed through the bathroom, joining her giggle. "Hands to yourself, Mr. Langston."

"I make no promises, Mrs. Langston." Alonzo helped her into the tub and then seated himself on the stool behind it.

As Lizzie settled in, she leaned back, and his hands found her shoulders, kneading lightly to relieve some of her stress. He made a note to himself to schedule her a spa appointment soon because if the tension in her shoulders was any indication, she certainly needed it.

"Why are you so good at that?" she moaned as she slid down just a bit deeper into the water.

"Lots of practice." She turned to shoot him another look, which only made him chuckle. "On you, princess. Only ever on you."

"And don't you forget it."

Alonzo hadn't just said that to placate her. It was the truth. Before he met Lizzie, things like running bubble baths, giving massages, and catering to a woman weren't in his usual repertoire. He never treated women poorly, he'd been raised better than that, but he never did anything that could have caused them to read more into their relationship than there really was. Like most people, he treated his twenties as a time of exploration. He fucked up and fucked around plenty. At that age, there wasn't much on his mind beyond making money and finding women to spend a few nights with. It made for a good time until it didn't.

He definitely didn't regret it, but he also knew that had he been that person when he met Lizzie, there was no way the two of them would be where they were today. By the time Lizzie walked into that community center, Alonzo had long grown tired of extremely late nights that turned into early mornings and had, much to Oliver's chagrin, been celibate for a little over a year. He'd been focusing on himself, building up the community, and figuring out what he wanted in the long run, and the answer he'd come to had been simple: he wanted a partner. What good was the money he'd made or the legacy built if he didn't have anyone to share it with? All of his friends—other than Oliver, of course —had begun to settle down with spouses and children to go home to every night, and meanwhile, he only had his latest client's portfolio to keep him warm at night.

That's not to say that he hadn't dated during that time because he had, but finding someone that held his attention beyond more than a few dates had been difficult. The women were sweet, beautiful, and driven, but none of them pulled at his heart. None of them made him feel that bolt of electricity he was looking for. Then, of course, explaining to them that, yes, at his big age, he was very much sticking to celibacy for a while received…interesting reactions, to say the least. Once he laid eyes on Lizzie, though, he suddenly understood why no one before her had ever worked out. The universe was just waiting for him to find her.

"Lost in thought back there?" Lizzie asked as she brought her wet fingers up and intertwined them with his.

"Maybe just a bit. I'm sorry, baby. What were you saying?"

Lizzie sat up, her skin glistening from the water, her breasts barely covered by the bubbles. "I asked whether or not you were going to climb in here with me before the water gets cold." The tone of her words matched the enticing look in her eyes, and he wanted to. God damn, did he want to, but instead of stripping, he simply leaned forward, one hand going to the back of her neck and pulling her to him for an exploratory kiss.

"Very tempting, baby, but I promised Monster I would read him a bedtime story and tuck him in," he said, using the nickname he'd given Christian what seemed like ages ago. Cookies were his favorite snack, so much so that he reminded them of Cookie Monster.

She let out a soft groan. "Why is it when you say things like that, it's both sweet and amazingly hot at the same damn time?"

"Just a curse, I guess."

Lizzie swatted at him, and after placing another quick kiss against her temple, he found his way out of their master bathroom and bedroom to head upstairs to Christian's room.

"Knock, knock, Monster." He stood on the threshold of the room, looking around until Christian came zooming out of his bathroom, toothbrush in hand.

"Brushing my teeth!"

At least, that was what Alonzo *thought* he said. It was sort of hard to tell with his mouth full of toothpaste the way it was. He raised an eyebrow as he watched his son's little feet carry him back into the bathroom to complete his routine. It didn't take long for him to finish, and a few minutes later, those same feet came barreling back into the room.

"Did you already grab a book from the shelf?"

Instead of answering, Christian climbed into the bed and pulled a book from under his pillow. Alonzo took a look at the cover and realized it was one of Christian's favorites, one about a little Black boy working to conquer his fear of the high diving board.

"Okay, let's settle in then." Christian did as he was told, fluffing his pillow while Alonzo pulled the desk chair next to the bed. "You read a page, I read a page?"

Christian nodded, opening the book, obviously ready to take the lead. Alonzo beamed with pride as he watched him read the first two pages. Even when he tripped over a few words, he kept going, sounding them out slowly, turning to look at Alonzo whenever he was a little unsure. Moments like these were the ones he loved the most.

They passed the book back and forth between them, and with each page they turned, he watched as his little Monster's eyes got lower and lower. With only a few pages left to go, Alonzo slowly slid the book from between his fingers once it was clear Christian was fast asleep. He put the book back in its place on the shelf and kissed him on his forehead as he pulled the covers over Christian. As he turned off the lights, Alonzo paused, taking a minute to enjoy the sight of him sleeping. Being that little boy's father was one of his biggest joys in life. It was going to take more than a blast from the past to change that.

CHAPTER 8

Lizzie

As the last customer of the day made their way out the door and Raven locked it behind them, Lizzie collapsed in her chair. *Long day* didn't even begin to cover it. "Okay, girl. I'm gonna hea—"

"Aht, aht! Don't even think about it. You're not going anywhere until we talk about what happened yesterday," Raven said, coming back over to settle into her own station chair. "I've been waiting for this all day." She shot Lizzie a look. "I held my tongue at book club yesterday because y'all had clearly figured it out and moved on, but *we*," she said, pointing her finger between the two of them, "need a debrief."

Lizzie released a breath. "King is back."

Nodding, Raven responded, "Mhmm, I figured that from all that hollering y'all were doing last night." Her concern shone through her eyes. "Why didn't you tell me, babe?"

"I don't knooow." She hated the whining quality her voice had taken on, but she couldn't help it. "The more people I tell, the more real it is. I haven't even really talked about it with anyone except Lonzo and then Morgan, obviously." It was the truth. Even though her sisters had been there when she'd gotten the call, she'd refused to talk about it after playing the message. Her phone had immediately been put back in her purse, and she'd practically begged them to just start the next movie so she could think about something else. *Anything else.*

"Okay, and I can understand that. You know I'm here for you, though, right? I love both you and Christian. I was there for the bullshit. Saw what he put you through. Now, no one can deny the fact that once he pulled the ultimate jackass move, you made shit work and did what had to be done. And yes, you've done an amazing job, mama, but I know how hard it's been."

Her words and penetrating stare caused tears to prick Lizzie's eyes. She really didn't want to cry. From the moment she'd first played that message, she'd been doing everything she could *not* to cry.

"So, if you say you're okay, I'll believe you, and we can both go about our business. If you say you're not ready to talk about it, then I'll leave you alone for now and let it go. Hell, I'll go hunt him and Morgan down to give them both the ass-whooping they deserve right quick. Just say the word. And if all you want to do is sit here and cry about it, we can do that, too. I'm here for whatever you need."

Apparently, Lizzie's instincts decided for her because it wasn't long before the tears began flowing down her face. True to her word, Raven immediately stood and came over to her, wrapping her arms around her as her shoulders began to shake. Sobs sounded throughout the shop as she finally thought about what she'd been through with King and did what she'd been trying to avoid for the last few days: fall apart.

———

"King! Where the fuck have you been? I've been calling you for hours!" Lizzie

yelled through clenched teeth as he finally made his way through the door of her hospital room. Another bolt of pain shot through her as she groaned.

"I got here as soon as I got Morgan's message, babe." He smiled and placed a kiss on her forehead.

"Which one?" The bite in her mother's voice made her cringe. Or maybe that was an after-effect of the contraction. Either way, the last thing she wanted to do was hear her mother tear King a new one because he was a little late for her labor.

A little? More like he'd already been out when she went into labor last night, only responding to text messages after Raven had already managed to get her to the hospital. When she'd first asked if he was on his way, he'd told her no, but she blamed herself for that one. Once she told him that she was nowhere near dilated, he'd convinced her that it didn't make sense for him to come up there for them both to be irritated and exhausted. Better he head home and get some rest so he could be fresh once things progressed, right? She'd hoped that meant that he would be at the hospital first thing in the morning, but that hadn't happened.

Now here they were, hours later, she was finally dilated enough to get the epidural, which she'd been literally begging for, and he was strolling in as if she wasn't in the process of trying to give birth to his big-headed ass baby.

Whatever. She didn't have the energy to fight about it. "It's fine, mommy. He's here now. That's all that matters."

Delilah huffed and cut her eyes at King. "I'm going to go find that damn nurse. Somebody should've been here by now to give you that epidural. They're gonna make me show my ass in this damn delivery wing if they keep playing with me."

She stalked out of the room, and King chuckled. "Damn, your mom is on one today, I see."

Lizzie closed her eyes as she tried to focus on her breathing. "She's just worried. We've been here all night, and I haven't gotten any sleep, and it's taken forever for me to get to six damn centimeters. The nurses would've sent me home last night, but my blood pressure kept dropping. She's just on edge."

Opening her eyes, she saw that King was barely paying attention to her, eyes focused on his phone instead of the mother of his child, who was clearly in pain.

"Did you hear anything I just said?"

"Huh? Oh, my bad," he said, finally glancing up from his phone. His face scrunched up at the sight of her glare. "What?"

"I'm sorry, is my giving birth interrupting your flourishing social life?"

The kiss of his teeth irritated her even more. "Here you go, trippin'. I'm here, aren't I? And from the looks of it, I didn't even have to rush over here because you're still not ready. Like, how much longer is this shit going to take?"

"Seriously? That's what you have to say to me? Not 'I'm so sorry I wasn't there when your water broke, babe.' Not 'How are you feeling?' or 'Do you need anything?'" Her voice broke as tears pooled in her eyes. "God, King, you can be a real asshole."

Tears began to fall down her face as she sniffled. This situation was stressful enough without King making things worse. "Bug, don't cry." He took a step closer to her and took her hand. "I'm sorry, okay. It's my bad that I haven't been here, but I'm here now. We're going to do this together. The doctor is going to come in, give you that shit that'll chill you out, and then before you know it, KJ is going to be here, and shit is going to be perfect."

Her lips formed a pout as he wiped away her tears. "I told you, we are not naming him after you. One King is all I can handle in my life."

The chuckle and smirk that she loved so much appeared, and she felt her heart skip a beat. She was just being emotional because of everything going on. He was right; hopefully, in a few hours, they'd be well on their way to being a happy little family.

"I finally found that damn nurse and she said the doctor is on her way." Delilah came into the room, both Makayla and Kendall trailing behind her, back from their trip to the cafeteria. True to her mother's word, the nurse and doctor came in ten minutes later and administered the epidural. As her contractions eased, so did the tension in the room. And in the end, it all really was worth it.

"Just one more push, Lizzie. You're doing great, mama," the doctor coached. With her mom on one side and King on the other, she gave it her all *and was finally rewarded with the cries of her baby boy. Exhaustion took over immediately as her head went crashing back into the pillow.*

"Oh, baby girl, he's beautiful," her mom said, emotion catching in her throat.

They placed him on Lizzie's chest, allowing the skin-to-skin contact she'd been so adamant about, and she couldn't find it in her to be bothered by his little wails. He really was beautiful. Her eyes found King, and she paused for just a moment, seeing his look of fear.

"Do you want to hold him, Daddy?" the nurse said, moving to pick him up.

His eyes went wide as he quickly shook his head. "Uh, no...go ahead and umm...clean him up first or whatever. I-I'm good." Was his voice shaking? If she'd had the strength, Lizzie would have laughed. King, with all his talk and bravado, was scared of a tiny ass baby. Who would have thought?

"You won't break him, you know."

He nodded absentmindedly, his eyes never leaving the newborn as the nurse carried him across the room to get him weighed and cleaned up. "I'm gonna go..." The words trailed off.

"King?"

Her voice seemed to snap him out of whatever daze he'd fallen into. "I'm going to go ahead and let everyone know he's here. I-I'll be back."

She nodded and watched him quickly disappear out of the room. Knowing the moment was probably just as overwhelming for him as it was for her, she decided not to worry, especially once the doctor told her they weren't quite finished yet.

Over the next day, any time someone asked King if he wanted to hold Christian, he said no. Lizzie didn't understand it. When he was in the room, he couldn't take his eyes off the little boy, but touching him was a whole other story.

"You know you're not going to break him, right?" she finally said to him as she placed Christian in the small clear bed beside her. She'd just finished another feeding, and he looked like he was drifting off to sleep.

"It's not that."

"Then what is it? The nurse showed you how to hold him, and you keep looking at him like you want to try. Why don't you?"

"Just working myself up to it, that's all. This shit is wild. It's…a lot."

Rolling her eyes as she leaned back in an attempt to get comfortable, Lizzie sighed. "Well, you're going to have to figure it out soon, daddy. Because after tomorrow, that little bundle of cuteness is coming home with us."

Lizzie didn't remember falling asleep, but she must have because the next thing she remembered was waking up to Raven comforting Christian in the chair next to her.

"Where's King?" Trying to stifle her yawn was pointless. A day and a half, and she was already tired as hell.

Raven shrugged. "No clue. He said something about needing to take care of something. Maybe getting stuff ready for tomorrow?"

It made sense. Knowing King, he hadn't thought to grab the car seat before heading to the hospital the first time. Asking Raven to pass her cell phone, she hit his contact ID. After about six rings, it went to voicemail. With a sigh, she tried again, only this time, it only took two rings before the automated message came through. On the third try, it didn't ring at all. She tried to tamp down the panic that started to stir in her chest. He was probably just in the shower. Better yet, he'd probably gotten home and fallen straight asleep. She could only imagine that he was almost as tired as she was, which was probably why he'd been acting strange. The man always was moody when he didn't get enough sleep.

Those same excuses played over and over again in her head as the after-noon and then the evening went on. Morgan, her sisters, her brother-in-law, her mom, Raven. They all came through the room, coming and going, cooing over Christian and checking on her to make sure she was fine. Every time someone walked through the door, she hoped it was King, but it never was. No one had seen or talked to him since he'd left the hospital. Everyone's phone calls went unanswered.

When Greg called to say he'd swung by the house but didn't come across King or his car, she started to get worried. What if something happened to him? When Greg called again and said that the car seat was still sitting at *the front door of the apartment, but it looked as though some of King's clothes were missing, she started to panic even more. And the next day, when it was Raven, Delilah, and Makayla who wheeled her from the room and out of the hospital, helping load her and Christian into the car, the tears started to fall, though she tried to keep the tightness in her chest at bay. King still wasn't answering his phone, and the silence around her read loud and clear. No one would say it aloud, but there was no doubt in her mind that her family was thinking the same thing as they helped her settle into her old bedroom at Delilah's house.*

There was only one reason why his clothes would be gone, things packed up in a rush, with the car missing. Only one plausible but highly inexcusable reason why he'd suddenly gone M.I.A., and no one had seen him since that second day in the hospital.

King was gone.

And as the reality of her situation hit her while she dialed his number over and over again with no change or response, she felt her heart breaking into a million little pieces. The tears blurred her vision until she couldn't see the screen of her phone anymore. The tightness in her chest worsened, and her breaths came in short spurts. She broke down right then and there as Christian's cries filled the house because it was finally clear that the perfect little family King had mentioned was never going to happen.

———

"It's okay, sis…I've got you," Raven whispered as she held her friend, bringing Lizzie back to the present, her sobs eerily similar to how they'd been all those years ago.

CHAPTER 9

Lizzie

"You seem anxious, Lizzie, and something tells me that you didn't request this emergency session because of anniversary planning or some exciting news at work."

Turns out that after spending several years together as therapist and client, Dr. Brunson really did know Lizzie. Who would've thought? That may have been why the slightly older Black woman's assistant had gotten back to her Monday afternoon to offer the Wednesday afternoon time slot Dr. Brunson typically reserved for her personal mindfulness sessions.

"You would be right about that one. Trust me when I say I wish this was about anniversary stress," Lizzie said with a weak smile.

"Did something happen with your sisters? I know you all had your monthly Sissas Only Night over the weekend."

"No, that actually went really well. For the most part, anyway. Though, I guess something that happened during that night is the reason why I'm here." The older woman nodded, waiting for her to continue, but all that followed was silence. When the words

"King contacted me" finally tumbled from her lips, it happened at just above a whisper.

The lack of surprise on Dr. Brunson's face was testament to not only her professionalism but also the women's long-standing relationship. This certainly wasn't the first time that she'd heard Christian's biological father's name. Dr. Brunson had been Lizzie's therapist for a little over five years. She'd seen her at her worst when she'd been dealing with sleepless nights, postpartum depression, and the devastating realization that her son's father had really abandoned them.

At the time, she was an overwhelmed single mom doing her best to keep things together and feeling as though she was failing miserably. Talking to her family and friends worked for a while, but it didn't take long for her to begin to worry she was burdening them with her mess when they had their own lives to think about. It also didn't help that talking to her mom or sisters meant having to listen to their opinions, which often felt like judgment whether they meant it that way or not. All she wanted was a safe space to work through her thoughts. It was actually Christian's pediatrician who'd suggested she look into therapy during his nine-month check-up.

So many people thought that going to therapy meant some-thing was wrong with you. Hell, Lizzie had the same notion for a very long time. Black families weren't exactly known for promoting the idea of mental health or wellness. After all, the old folks did live by the words "dirty laundry belongs in the home, not out in the streets."

Because of that thought process, therapy certainly didn't come easy. She went through her worries about saying the wrong thing and the fear that she was wasting both of their time. She didn't even start out with Dr. Brunson—or Kiera, as she insisted Lizzie call her. She'd tried out a few sessions with two or three other therapists and was just about ready to give up the idea of the whole thing when she came across the middle-aged Black woman just striking out into her own practice. The highs, the lows. She'd helped Lizzie through it all, including the decision to not only love herself, but fall in love with Alonzo as well, and Lizzie would be forever grateful to Dr. Brunson for that.

"Wow," she said, pulling Lizzie from her thoughts. "That must have been off-putting as hell."

Lizzie let out a snort. "That's one way of putting it."

"And how would you put it?"

"I just about shit bricks."

They both laughed at that, an ease settling through the room. "Okay, I can definitely understand that. Seems like an appropriate response when you get that sort of shock. But I know you can articulate your feelings a bit better than that," Kiera said as she raised an eyebrow.

The words came to her easily, more than likely because she'd been working through her feelings from the moment she'd first listened to the message. "I definitely feel off balance. I'm supposed to be focused on celebrating my marriage and the home we've built together, and instead, I'm stressing out about an asshole who left me and his son high and dry years ago. I'm happy, healthy, successful, and loved, then suddenly, I get one little phone call, and the world feels like it's upside down."

"Sounds like you're giving some of your power away." She leaned toward Lizzie, her words firm but gentle. "You make it sound like you've only been happy because he hasn't been around. And you know as well as I do that even though Alonzo makes you a very happy woman, your relationship with him isn't the reason you're happy or whole, either. You're all of those things you mentioned because you put in the work to get yourself there."

Lizzie knew her therapist was right. She'd spent countless hours working on herself both inside of this office and out. She'd done what was necessary to save herself after realizing she'd spent so much time waiting for her knight in shining armor to come and do it for her. By the time she met Alonzo, she hadn't been some damsel in distress waiting in the tower for him to save her from heartbreak or give her a fairytale ending. She'd done that for herself. Alonzo being able to add to her life and contribute to her happy ending was just a very well-deserved bonus.

"Are you afraid?"

Lizzie's eyes stayed on her hands as she gave a quick nod, her breathing a little shallow. Her fear might be obvious, but that didn't make it any easier to admit.

"Can you tell me what you're afraid of? Take a minute if you need to."

Lizzie thought for a moment, running through all the surface-level fears that came to mind first. It would have been easy to list one of them, but easy wasn't what Kiera was looking for. It's not what would help Lizzie right now. So instead, she voiced the fear she'd been working overtime to ignore.

"I think what I'm most afraid of is seeing him and turning back into that girl I was when he left. The one who was scared, alone, and for whatever reason, not enough to make him stay. And I'm afraid that letting him back in won't only do that to me but turn Christian into someone who thinks he's not enough either."

Kiera nodded. "Anything else?"

"It feels selfish to say, but honestly…I'm afraid of having to share Christian with King."

"I think it's perfectly natural for a mama bear to want to protect her cub."

"That's not it. I mean, yes, of course, I want to protect him. I want to wrap him up so that nothing ever hurts him, especially when it comes to King, but I'm talking about actually sharing Christian with him. I know it sounds selfish as hell, but there's part of me that just doesn't want to have to start including him in our lives. Alonzo is the only father Christian has ever known.

What does this look like if King actually is back for good? When suddenly, I have to deal with the fact that not only does King actually want to spend time with him and get to know him, but Christian wants the same thing? When it's not just me that he has to spend holidays and birthdays with or showing up to Tae Kwon Do or basketball and soccer games. When I have to look at and interact with King on a regular basis." Lizzie took a deep breath and shook her head. "I don't know what's more terrifying. The thought that he'll leave Christian heartbroken or the thought that I'll be forced to accept him back into my life again."

There, she'd said it. It felt completely self-centered, but it was true. She'd vowed a long time ago that if Christian's dad ever came back into the picture, she wouldn't keep him from their son. She never wanted to give Christian a reason to resent her for doing something like that, and she knew she'd never forgive herself if she did. Still, that didn't stop her from wanting to be selfish. She knew she'd never go through with it, not unless King gave her a reason, but damn it, she wished she could just say fuck him and forget he'd ever called her.

When she finally looked up at Kiera, the woman was smiling. "What?"

"I'm proud of you."

Lizzie let out a snort. "Why, because I'm admitting to being a bit of a selfish bitch?"

"Because you let yourself be honest, out loud, even though you thought it was something that would make you look bad. That you said how you were really feeling, even though it opened you up to judgment. It's not about being selfish or not. It's about the fact that a few years ago, you would've never dreamed of acknowledging that side of you. Not to yourself, and certainly not to me or anyone else."

Lizzie nodded, her own small smile forming.

"And let's be honest. Those are some complicated ass feelings that you're working through. None of the scenarios in front of you right now are going to be easy, and it's okay to admit that. Full disclosure, you already have the tools, support, and strength that you need to get through this. I know it feels like you have to have all the answers right now, but don't put that pressure on yourself. And don't let anyone else put it on you, either. Navigate this on your own timetable, whatever that means and whatever that looks like. And remember, just like you have the power and ability to decide what's right for you, it's important that Christian understands that he's able to do the same. He needs to have a sense of agency in this as well."

"You're right. I know you're right. It's why you get paid the big bucks," she said playfully.

As they moved through the rest of the session, their initial conversation never strayed too far from Lizzie's mind. As much as she wanted to place King in the same box he'd always been in, the truth was, she didn't know who he was now, and it wouldn't be fair for her to assume that she did. She would need to face this head-on, and Christian needed to be an active party in making this decision. He deserved a fair shot at getting to know King if that's what he wanted.

The last thing she wanted was to have her power taken away and so she would do what she could to extend that same courtesy to everyone else involved.

CHAPTER 10

Alonzo

The Thursday night meet-up at Titan could not come soon enough for Alonzo. Typically, he found his comfort either looking into his wife's eyes or diving between her legs, but tonight called for a different sort of stress relief. As the taste of cognac filled his senses, he closed his eyes and allowed himself to bask in the glory of it. It didn't matter what anyone said, the yak just hit different.

"You didn't hear a damn thing Oliver just said, did you?" chuckled Reggie.

"I try not to make it a habit to pay attention to anything that he says outside of business hours," Alonzo said, his own deep chuckle leaving his chest.

"Don't even try it, Lonzo. Your ass is probably just over there having some type of spiritual experience off one sip of cognac," Oliver threw back at him.

"I've heard good liquor and a great cigar can do that for a nigga." Alonzo tipped his glass in the direction of Reggie's friend, Lucas, agreeing with his words. He hadn't spent a lot of time with the younger man, but he made an effort to include him whenever the group got together.

Every man needed a tight circle. In a world that, more often than not, wanted to chew Black men up and spit them out, it was essential to have a safe space with people you not only trusted but could turn to when you needed them. That was a lesson that Alonzo had learned over his lifetime, and he was glad to be able to say that he'd found that in all the men present. His eyes drifted over toward his brother-in-law, Greg. He knew the other man could benefit from leaning on the group a bit more but also didn't think it was his place to push him into that. Not just yet, at least. Besides, he had his own shit that he needed to work through.

"Yo, Greg. You good over there?" Even if he didn't want to push him, it didn't hurt to ask.

"Yeah. Thanks for reaching out. I don't know about the rest of y'all, but I definitely needed this night off." He took a gulp of the barrel-aged beer that the owner had recommended.

"I heard that. The stress is real out here."

"Nigga, please," Lucas groaned. "I don't think I've seen you the least bit stressed since you got with Makayla. I didn't think you could be more chill than you already were, but shorty proved me wrong."

"What can I say? Baby girl makes me happier than I've ever been." The pride on Reggie's face said it all.

"This nigga." The group laughed at Lucas's grumbling. Truth be told, Alonzo knew the same was true for Makayla. His sister-in-law had always been a bit of a spitfire, but she had a glow about her lately that could only be attributed to how happy the younger man made her.

"What have I told you about hating on my shit?" Reggie shot back. "Besides, it's not my fault that you've never known the love of a Michaels woman. They are a different breed, okay."

"Here, here," Alonzo said, tipping his own glass. Out of the corner of his eye, he saw Greg make the same motion, though he wasn't sure if he meant it for better or for worse.

"Yeah, well, I tried to get in on that Michaels woman love, but Lonzo was being stingy as fuck. It's bad enough that he hooked you up with my baby Makayla, but he played me to the left about Ms. Delilah, too. He didn't want to have to answer to me as his father-in-law. I just know I could've made Ms. Delilah a happy woman." Oliver was a whole ass clown.

"Trust me, bruh. You couldn't handle her, no matter how hard you tried."

The group couldn't help but laugh because they all knew how much of a handful Delilah could be. That wasn't to say she wasn't a sweetheart because she certainly was, but she certainly didn't make things easy for Percy. The older man never seemed to complain, though, which had to count for something.

"Fool shit aside, you good, man? You look like you've got some shit on your mind?"

Leave it to Reggie to notice. He always was an observant brother. It was one of the reasons that Alonzo valued his opinion so much. "Some shit is going on at home, and I'll be honest, I'm at a loss for how to handle this situation."

It'd been days since Lizzie played the message from King for him in their kitchen. Not quite a week but close enough, and Alonzo had yet to stop hearing the other man's voice and request. It played on a loop in his head over and over again. Just the thought of it made him want to throw something.

Reggie stood and gestured for Alonzo to follow him out onto the deck connected to their cigar room. Though they didn't mind sitting in the main lounge area, the owner, D'Angelo, often gave them one of his private rooms whenever they requested it. The two men closed the sliding glass door behind them, leaving the others to their jokes.

"I figured you may want some privacy for this conversation.

Hope I'm not overstepping," Reggie said, taking a sip of the bourbon in his glass. "I know we're not as close as you and Oliver, but…" He shrugged. "I'm here to listen if you want to talk."

There was some truth to the other man's words. Alonzo and Reggie weren't best friends, but he did consider the younger man a close friend. He knew if he brought this situation to Oliver, he would put his joking aside long enough to help him figure things out, but he also didn't know if it was appropriate to broach this subject with him. They may have been friends for decades, but this was his wife's business, which meant for right now, letting Oliver know wasn't an option. Reggie, on the other hand?

"Did Makayla happen to mention anything about their girls' night from Friday?" he asked cautiously. He already knew that both of Lizzie's sisters knew what was going on since they'd been there when she'd gotten the call. And while Alonzo was ninety-nine percent certain that Kendall hadn't mentioned shit about it to Greg since the two barely seemed to be coexisting at this point, he was less certain about what Makayla may have done or said.

Reggie gave a slow nod. "You mean about Lizzie's ex calling her out of fucking nowhere? Yeah, trust me when I say I got an earful once baby girl made it back home. I don't know, bruh, but I'll just say he better hope that Makayla never gets eyes on him 'cause it's definitely on sight." He let out a chuckle. "And we both know that's some scary ass shit."

That only made Alonzo chuckle right along with him. One of the things he loved most about his sister-in-law was that she never held her tongue and had absolutely no cut cards. So yeah, he knew without a doubt that if she ever saw King Holden, it'd be in King's best interest to run for his life.

"Phone call have you spooked?" Reggie asked.

"More like pissed the fuck off." He let out a sigh, shaking his head. "And I don't even know if I really have the right to be."

"From what I hear, you definitely have a right to be. Asshole shows up out of the blue all these years later, suddenly wanting to make nice, disrupting your life, Lizzie's life, and your son's life? I'm pretty sure anyone in your situation would be more than pissed off." The silence hung between them before Reggie broke it again. "Have you and Lizzie talked about what you're going to do?"

He nodded. "She's going to meet with him." After coming home from her appointment with Dr. Brunson, Lizzie let him know that she'd decided to meet with King and hear him out. Alonzo was sure that he was going to break a few teeth, he'd been clenching so damn hard. He made it a point not to ask for details about what went on during her therapy sessions. As far as he was concerned, those were her private moments, and he wouldn't intrude on them unless she wanted to offer up details. From what he gathered, she'd gotten what she needed from the session and came back with a clear head. He could tell that she was still hesitant about meeting with King, but she reassured him that, at the very least, she should hear what he had to say for Christian's benefit.

"She said she owes it to Christian to see if King really has what it takes to step up and be in his life."

"And you don't agree?" Leave it to Reggie to pose the hard question.

"It's not that I don't agree, it's that I do. That's part of what makes me so damn mad. As much as I want to say fuck him and the horse he's trying to ride in on and no matter how justified I may be for wanting to do that, I know that she's right. Christian should know his father if that's what he wants." Even saying it aloud made Alonzo's blood boil.

"I'll say this, Lonzo, you are a far better man than I am. Must come with old age."

"You ain't shit," Alonzo said with a laugh, the small dig breaking the tension of their conversation.

"That's probably true." Reggie laughed along with him. "But

seriously, man, if you remember anything, remember this: it takes more than making a baby to be a parent. King may have helped create Christian, but you're the parent who raised him. That's your little boy. He won't ever forget that, so you make sure you don't either." With that, Reggie left Alonzo on the deck to his own thoughts.

CHAPTER 11

Lizzie

Lizzie showed up at the Cream + Sugar Cafe twenty minutes early. She told herself not to, did everything she could to ignore the compulsion, and yet, she still showed up early. Damn her mother for instilling her with home training and damn her for actually following it. Of course, being early meant that she was left waiting for King to show up for a total of thirty minutes. She should've known better. He never could get anywhere on time. And just like she remembered, when he finally strolled in, he did it as if he had all the time in the damn world.

"Damn, Bug," he said, approaching the corner table. "You look...good."

"And you're late," she said, clearly unamused. Her eyes scanned over him. Not much had changed since she'd last seen him. King Holden was the definition of a light-skinned devil—at least that's what her mama always said—with a close-cut fade, eyes that couldn't decide if they wanted to be hazel or green, and light brown skin that always tended to freckle whenever he was in the sun too long. Only difference between now and then was the facial hair that adorned his once-smooth face.

He chuckled and took a seat. "My bad. I didn't mean to keep you waiting, but I meant what I said. You look damn good. Short hair suits you." He flashed her the smile that used to make her weak in the knees. Now, all it did was make her nauseous. "How have you been?"

"How about you ask me how your son has been?" *You know, considering you've never even met him,* she thought to herself.

That smile didn't even move an inch. "Touché. You're right. We can start there if you want." Like he was doing her some sort of favor. "So, how *has* he been?"

Lizzie wished she could fight it, but a genuine smile spread across her face. "He's doing really well. Just started the first grade, which means he can start playing sports now. He wants to join both the soccer team and the basketball team at his school for first and second graders. Literally can't stop talking about it. Gotta admit, it's driving us all up the wall." She let out a laugh.

"Basketball team, huh? I guess I shouldn't be surprised. After all, it is in his genes."

Well, that certainly wiped the smile right off of her face. Leave it to King to point out that Christian got his enthusiasm for basketball honestly. As if she really needed him to remind her. It was one of the first things to cross Lizzie's mind when her baby boy first came home to tell her and Alonzo about the team. For as long as Lizzie and King had known each other, he'd loved basketball. Swore he would go pro, but much like the walking cliché he was, a torn ACL had killed that dream.

"We're not here to go down memory lane, King."

"You sure? Honestly, I thought that was exactly why we were here, Bug." He leaned forward, his hand reaching across the table toward hers. Lizzie snatched it away, placing both hands in her lap, the intimacy of his attempt causing her stomach to turn.

"Please don't touch me. And don't call me that."

King leaned back and raised both hands. "My bad, I didn't mean any disrespect. You know me, I've always been a physical touch type of person." He paused. "Didn't think you'd mind since you never seemed to before."

"Yeah, well, these days, I value my personal space and boundaries." It was one of the standards that therapy had helped her develop. She was in control of her life, her body, and herself. She had the right to establish that in any way and to whoever she deemed necessary. The surprised look on King's face wasn't lost on her. She'd been quiet when they were together. Not necessarily a doormat, but Lizzie had hardly ever stood up for herself. He'd never been outright physically cruel or abusive to her, but his big personality and wants usually overshadowed hers. Those days were long gone. He was meeting the new and improved Lizzie, something he obviously hadn't been expecting. "Like I said, I'm not here to reminisce with you."

"Guess I just had this all the way fucked up, huh?" He chuckled, but if she was reading him correctly, he wasn't all that amused. "So, why are you here then? Call me naive, but I thought it was because you wanted to see an old friend. Someone you cared about once upon a time and maybe still do. Or is that just me pushing my own shit onto you?"

The heat crept up Lizzie's neck as she felt herself get more and more frustrated. She should've known this would happen. King always loved to play games. Make things into something that they weren't. He'd practically made a talent of getting under her skin years ago. Some things really didn't change.

"I'm here because, despite my best judgment, I decided to give you a chance and see if you'd grown up at all. Silly me for thinking that this might actually be about you wanting to see your child after all these years. Maybe make an attempt at being in his life like a real adult." Lizzie noticed the tick of his jaw as he looked away from her. She'd definitely struck a nerve.

"Maybe I wanted to see both of y'all. Make a connection with both him and you and show you that I actually have changed," he finally said after a minute or so of silence.

Lizzie held up her left hand, her wedding ring set catching the light. "This," she said, pointing directly to her gold wedding band, "pretty much nullifies whatever you *thought* was going to happen between the two of us. If you're not here to discuss Christian, then we have nothing to talk about." She moved to stand and leave, but he grabbed her hand to stop her. The look she shot him must've been fit to kill, considering how quickly he let go.

"Personal space. Right, my bad." King let out a breath and scrubbed his hand over his face. "Morgan did mention something about you being married. Must've slipped my mind." He chuckled. "Guess I can't say that I'm surprised someone saw the same thing in you that I saw when we first got together." He looked up at her. "Bu– I mean Lizzie, can you just…can you sit down? Please? I promise I'll be on my best behavior from now on."

Lizzie eyed him suspiciously but did as he asked. She'd come here to give him a chance, and that's what she intended to do. "You are really testing the little patience I have left, King." She felt like she was being herded toward the edge of a cliff, and he was two seconds from pushing her right over. She'd managed to hold her own and stand her ground, but on the inside, she was flustered. She was fraying bit by bit and beginning to feel trapped in the small coffee shop.

"I know, I know. Guess I still have that complex where I think any attention is better than no attention at all, even when it's not all that great." This time when he leaned in, he didn't make any move to touch her. "All bullshit aside, I really do want to see Christian, maybe get to know him if that's okay with you? I'm going to be in town for the next few weeks and… Well, shit, it's been weighing on me lately that I have a whole son out there that I don't even know."

"And whose fault is it that you don't know him, King? Certainly not mine."

"No, not yours. That's all on me. Trust me when I say that I know that. I know I fucked up when I left and then fucked up again by not coming back. I'm just asking you to give me the opportunity to show you that I'm ready to do something different."

She was quiet for a while, contemplating what he'd said. As much as Lizzie hated to admit it, King seemed sincere. She didn't doubt that he was any less full of shit than he had been when he'd walked in to meet with her, but the look in his eyes suggested that maybe he really did want to change the way things were.

"Is it okay if I think about it?" He moved to say something, and she raised a hand to stop him. "I heard you. I *hear* you. I-I'm not saying no. I'm just saying that this isn't something I can give you an answer on right now. And honestly, it's not a decision I should really make on my own."

King kissed his teeth and looked away, the tick in his jaw making another appearance. "Damn. So what, your nigga gets to say whether or not I get to meet my son?" he snapped. "You can't keep him from me, Lizzie."

"First of all, watch your tone. Talking to me like that isn't going to make me do whatever you want me to. Second, no, Alonzo doesn't get to make the final decision, but he *will* be a part of this conversation, and he has a right to know what you're asking for because he's part of Christian's life. The operative word you used was 'meet.' You're just now trying to meet Christian, and Alonzo has been in his life for a long time. Don't get it twisted. You're the interloper here, not him. Third, at the end of the day, this is a decision that Christian is going to have to make. This is going to affect *him* more than anyone else, so I want to know what he is and isn't comfortable with."

"His decision?" His eyes finally made their way back to her face instead of roaming around the room to avoid looking at her. "He's six."

"Yes, and he's a whole person with thoughts, feelings, and opinions. I'm not going to take his choices away from him just because of his age. I'm not that type of parent, and if you're going to be in his life, you're going to have to learn not to be either." She took a deep breath and counted back from five to calm herself down. "I'm not trying to keep him from you. I'm just trying to figure out the best way to navigate this without completely upending his life and mine."

Lizzie expected him to give her more pushback, but King surprised her by conceding, giving her a nod. Ready to end the conversation, she stood up, and this time, thankfully, he didn't try to stop her. "Once I have everything figured out, I'll call you and let you know."

"Bet." Soon that cocky smirk of his returned as he stood up with her. "Is it safe to assume that a hug is out of the question?" She shot him a look that said *don't even try it.* "Fair enough. Can't blame a man for trying."

"I'm sure I could," she grumbled, adjusting her purse on her shoulder.

"At the risk of you snapping on me, I gotta say, Lizzie, it really was good seeing you." His gaze traveled the length of her body, and she had to fight not to roll her eyes. "Really good."

"Bye, King," Lizzie said, refusing to acknowledge his comment. It took everything in her to keep her calm as she walked toward the door when all she really wanted to do was bolt so that she could get the hell out of Dodge and quickly.

She may have managed to get away home free this time, but it was obvious that King wouldn't be going anywhere any time soon.

CHAPTER 12

Alonzo

Alonzo cleared his throat as his phone gave a little buzz in his pocket. He hoped it was Lizzie letting him know that she was on her way to meet him at their anniversary venue. He'd already been there for a little over twenty minutes, and while he'd been able to push back both his client meetings for the afternoon, he didn't want to take up more of Dana and Malcolm Davis's time than necessary. Midnight Trail was the perfect place to hold their anniversary party, considering Lizzie's love of most things country music. They'd ironed out the initial details, but there were a few more things they wanted to discuss.

Quickly reading over his wife's message, he let the couple know that she would be there in no more than a few minutes. They smiled in understanding, letting him know to head on back to the office area once she arrived. There were two weeks left before their anniversary, and all Alonzo wanted was for everything to be perfect. He wasn't sure how likely that was considering the recent bit of chaos that had emerged, but he was doing his best to support Lizzie however he could.

"I am so, so, so sorry I'm late!" the woman in question said, sprinting into the room. "Everything just sort of got thrown off after I met with King earlier, and my schedule went completely to hell." Her words came out in a rush, and Alonzo couldn't help but smile at how cute she was when she was flustered.

Taking a few steps to close the distance between them, he brought his hands to either side of her face, cupping her cheeks. "You know, it would probably be a great idea to actually take a breath between words. Otherwise, we'll have to explain to Dana why you passed out in the middle of their dance floor."

"Don't be cute," she said, poking him in the chest, though the twinkle in her eye said that she was at least slightly amused by his words.

"Right. I forgot that's your job." He leaned down, capturing her lips with his for a kiss. "Better?"

"A little," she answered with a small smile. Alonzo placed a kiss against her temple before taking a step back. "I really am sorry."

"Don't worry about it, princess. Today has just been one of those days." He took her hand in his. "Ready to get started?"

Lizzie immediately lit up. "Yes, yes, and yes!"

The two of them headed back toward the office, finding the door open and both Dana and Malcolm waiting for them. After assuring Lizzie that there were no apologies necessary, the couple took them through their ideas for the party.

"So, Alonzo was telling us that you were thinking of making this a casual event?" Dana asked, her notebook in her hands so that she could take notes.

"Mhmm. I was telling my sisters that I wanted this to be like a Black honky-tonk. Cowboy boots and hats, plenty of whiskey and beer to go around, line dancing, good barbecue, the works."

"Sounds like my kind of party." Everyone in the room laughed, but it was clear they all agreed.

"I know Lonzo mentioned that we might be able to use the in-house chef?"

"Not a problem at all." That came from Malcolm. "We actually talked to him a bit, and he had a few ideas on food but said that for anything specific that you may or may not want, just let him know. The only thing he was concerned about was desserts."

"Oh, you don't have to worry about that. My sister's best friend has that under control. She has her own catering business specifically geared toward desserts, and we plan to exploit her talent while also paying her well." In truth, it hadn't taken much to convince Jasmine to handle that part of the event. After all, she was family, and she was always looking for more exposure.

"Oh, great! Would you mind leaving her information? That way, we can see if there's anything she needs from us."

"Of course!"

"What my wife isn't telling you is that she also wants to grill her to see if she'd be interested in the possibility of partnering with us. We've been looking around for pastry chefs or local bakers to feature on the menu." Malcolm cut his eyes over to Dana, who gave him a wink.

"Trust me, Jas won't have any problem with that."

The rest of the meeting went well. The group covered ambiance and decorations, music, and entertainment, and even went around the venue to decide what should be placed where. By the time everything was all said and done, they had pretty much everything squared away and figured out. Alonzo and Lizzie still needed to finalize the menu, but he promised the Davises that they'd have that information within the next couple of days. If the woman he loved wanted to celebrate their anniversary with a couple yeehaws, he was going to make sure that's exactly what they did.

———

Alonzo cleared his throat as the two of them settled into bed. After discussing the party plans, finishing up their workdays, and then making it back home to cook dinner as a family and put Christian to bed, he knew they were both beyond exhausted. Still, there was one thing left to talk about. He'd managed to avoid the topic earlier, but it seemed now was as good a time as any to broach the subject. "So, how did everything go with King?"

Lizzie rolled her eyes as she leaned back into his chest. "As well as can be expected, I guess. In some ways, he's the same exact person he always was. Thinks he can win anyone over with his bullshit and a smile."

Of course. Alonzo had never had the pleasure of meeting King, but he'd heard enough about him not to have a high opinion of the other man. "Sounds like he still has some growing up to do."

"That's an understatement," she said with a sigh. "But...as much as I hate to admit it, I think he's sincere about wanting to meet Christian and getting to know him. He says he'll be here for a few weeks. I can't say for sure that he'll stick around this time like he says, but I think he at least deserves the benefit of the doubt. I told him as much, though I did ultimately say it would be up to Christian."

Alonzo could tell that even saying that aloud took its toll on her. He must've been silent for a beat too long because Lizzie turned around to face him. "Are you...are you okay with that?"

"I'm okay with moving forward however you think is best."

This time her eye roll was directed at him. "Don't do that, Lonzo."

His eyebrows furrowed in confusion. "Don't do what?"

"That thing you do where instead of telling me how you really feel, you tell me what you think I want to hear. Or better yet, you give me the 'appropriate answer' instead of the truth."

"Now, wait a minute because I've never lied to you. You know that." He was conscious not to snap at her or raise his voice, but he resented what she seemed to be implying.

"Okay, and I'm not saying you have, so you can pump your brakes on that thought. All I'm saying is sometimes you're extra cautious with what you say. And while I appreciate the fact that you don't want to overstep and you're trying to be conscious of my feelings right now, tiptoeing around the subject or trying to placate me is not what I need right now. This is not a backseat type of situation. Tell me how you really feel."

Well, shit. Consider him properly scolded, then. Honestly, he didn't really mind because he knew Lizzie was right. She knew better than anyone that even though he knew just how well she could take care of herself, that never stopped him from taking on the role of her protector whether she needed him to or not. He may not always go about it in the best way, but he never had ill intentions. He knew, though, that wasn't the only reason why he'd been keeping his feelings under wraps.

"You're sure?" She nodded without hesitation. Okay, then. "I think, no, I know that it's going to take some time getting used to the idea of King being around. We've got the parenting thing on lock, and the slightly less evolved side of me is fighting real hard not to beat my chest at that nigga and tell him we've got this. I know that's not fair to Christian, though, so I get it. And I can't promise that I'm gonna always be able to hold my tongue when he's around, but I'm going to do my best. I'm trying to let you drive this car because I do honestly believe that what you and Monster want comes first here. Above how I feel and above what I think."

"But you do realize that what you feel and think matters too, right? I don't parent him alone, baby. He's your son just as much as he is mine, and you know I'm not just saying that because of the adoption. None of that is any less true just because King might be coming back into the picture."

After Alonzo proposed, amongst all the bells and wedding

planning, the two of them talked at length about him adopting Christian. Alonzo had been the one to bring it up, testing the waters and asking Lizzie how she felt about it. It had surprised him a bit when she said that she wasn't quite sure how ready she was for that step, but he'd understood. She explained how, as much as she loved the idea, part of her was still holding onto the hope that King would come back wanting to be a father to Christian. Logically, they both knew that Alonzo being his legal father didn't bar King from being a parent, but they'd also agreed to give it some time and revisit the conversation later.

About six months after they were married, they discussed it again, only this time it was Lizzie who broached the topic, saying she didn't want to put any of their lives on hold for someone who clearly didn't want to be there any longer. Alonzo had been ecstatic, though he'd always made it clear that Christian was his child, piece of paper or not. Still, being able to give the little boy his last name brought him a sense of joy he couldn't find words to explain. The adoption went smoothly since King had disappeared without signing the birth certificate, which meant he never had any real parental rights to give up, and they didn't have to try and track him down to get his permission. To be honest, once everything was all said and done, Alonzo always wondered how the other man would take it if he ever decided to come around. He guessed he would be finding out soon.

"Logically, I know that, but like, I'm having a difficult time getting that to resonate."

His favorite mischievous grin appeared on her lips as Lizzie sat up on her knees and used a hand to guide him back against the headboard. "Well, tell your inner caveman that I'm here to remind him who's the actual king of this castle any time he needs me to." She hiked up the bottom of her sleep dress just enough to help herself position her knees on either side of his hips until she was straddling him.

"Is that so?" he asked, his hands finding their way up the

back of her exposed thighs until he had a firm grip on her plump ass. Just the feel of her cheeks in his hands had him harder than a motherfucker, and he wasn't about to complain.

"Absolutely."

"Well, princess…seems to me that I may need a little reminder right about now." He thrust his hips up, and the whimper that escaped her lips turned him on even more.

"I think that can be arranged."

CHAPTER 13

Lizzie

"Christian, daddy and I have something we want to talk to you about."

Talking to Christian together was an automatic decision for both Alonzo and Lizzie. The when and where was a little difficult for them to pin down, but they eventually decided that a visit to their favorite pop-up dessert truck was the perfect backdrop for their conversation. They would be able to grab his favorite treat and tell him in a relaxed situation while also getting it out of the way before they went to her mom and Percy's house the next day for the monthly Sunday dinner. Lizzie had been avoiding having this conversation with her mother until they'd made a decision on what to do, but she knew she couldn't hold off any longer. Knowing her sisters, namely Kendall, the tea had already been spilled, which meant it was only a matter of time before she was bombarded with questions.

"Am I in trouble?" Christian asked cautiously, his eyes narrowing as he stopped right in the middle of digging his spoon into his triple fudge sundae.

"Should you be?" Lizzie asked. She raised an eyebrow,

suddenly suspicious of what her baby boy had been up to that prompted that question. He quickly shook his head. "Then no, you're not in trouble," she laughed.

After taking a quick peek at Alonzo, who reached over and gave her hand a supportive squeeze, she cleared her throat and pushed on. "Do you remember how Cousin Morgan is family?"

Christian nodded. "She's cousins with my birth dad…right?"

"Right," she said with a small smile. "Do you remember his name?" Christian stared down at his ice cream for a bit before shaking his head.

"That's okay. I know we don't talk about him much." The last thing Lizzie wanted was for her baby boy to feel bad about not remembering. She wasn't lying when she said they didn't talk about King often. Really, they didn't talk about him much at all. "His name is King. King Holden."

Christian put down his spoon and tucked his hands into his lap. It took more than a bit of effort for Lizzie not to laugh at the way he furrowed his brow, putting on his serious face. She noticed the smirk on Alonzo's face and knew he was thinking the same thing.

"How would you feel about…" She stopped, the words getting caught in her throat. Suddenly, she couldn't get them out.

"How would you feel," Alonzo said, picking up where she left off, "about meeting your birth dad?" Lizzie looked at her husband and gave him a grateful smile. This time she was the one giving his hand a squeeze.

"Meet him? How?" The confusion on Christian's face was clear.

"Well, he's here in town. He called your mom and wants to see you. Maybe spend some time together so you can get to know each other? What do you think about that?"

Lizzie watched as the realization of what Alonzo was saying sank in. The butterflies in her stomach were going into overdrive, waiting for his answer. When she noticed the tell-tale wobble of Christian's bottom lip set in, she started to panic.

Quickly slipping out of her chair, she made her way around the table and kneeled in front of him. "Chris, baby, it's okay! If this isn't something you want to do, we won't be upset, I promise."

Alonzo leaned forward, placing his hand on the back of Christian's neck, something that always seemed to calm him down. "Your mom's right, Monster. It's okay if you're not ready or you're not sure about this."

"It's not that," Christian sniffled. "What if...what if he meets me and decides he doesn't like me?"

Now it was Lizzie's turn to get emotional. "Baby, is that what you're worried about?" She leaned forward and pressed the biggest kiss possible on his forehead. "Baby boy, he is going to love you just as much as your dad and I do. I promise."

"But how do you know?"

"Because any other possibility is out of the question," said Alonzo. He stood and bent down to place his own kiss on top of Christian's head. "In fact, it's just scientifically impossible for him not to love you."

"But—"

"No buts," Lizzie smiled. "Trust us. We're the experts here." She shot him a wink that finally brought a small smile to his little face.

Once she was sure that he was okay, Lizzie slid back into her seat. They spent the next few minutes answering Christian's other questions about when and where he would get to meet King and how long he would be around. That last one was a little tricky to answer, so she simply told him that King would be around for as long as he could. By the end, she could tell that Christian was getting excited. He did have one more concern, though.

"Daddy...if I start to see my other dad more, does that mean you'll have to stop being my dad?" Damn, this little boy knew just how to hit her right in the feels.

"Of course not." His answer came without an ounce of hesitation, not that Lizzie expected anything less. "I will always be your dad. Nothing could or would ever change that, you hear me? This just means now, you're lucky enough to have two dads loving and looking out for you."

Christian seemed satisfied by that answer and quickly switched subjects, telling them about the game of tag he'd managed to win at recess the day before. As they listened to him tell the story with a mouth full of ice cream, two things crossed Lizzie's mind.

The first was that it was going to be hell trying to get the chocolate stains out of his shirt. The second was how she would absolutely beat the entire shit out of King if he broke her baby's heart.

CHAPTER 14

Alonzo

Sunday dinner at his mother-in-law's house was admittedly one of Alonzo's favorite days of the month. Both he and Lizzie knew their way around the kitchen, but neither of them had anything on Delilah. The way that woman threw down in the kitchen needed to be studied, bottled, and sold in all fifty states. She usually sent out the menu beforehand in case anyone had any notes or restrictions for that month. Nine times out of ten, no one had any complaints or requests, and he knew today's menu would be no different. There wasn't a person alive who could resist Delilah's golden fried chicken, especially when it was paired with garlic mashed potatoes, crispy glazed Brussels sprouts, yeast rolls, and topped off with her specialty citrus pound cake. Yeah, he was fittin' to eat good today.

"Look at you over there like a kid in a candy store!" Lizzie giggled as they pulled into the driveway. "I swear you're worse than Christian." His grown ass was practically bouncing in the driver's seat.

"Don't be a hater, baby. You're way too beautiful for that." He turned off the car and climbed out, jogging to the other side to open her door. "Besides, my mouth has been drooling all day thinking about getting a taste of that pound cake."

"Oh, is that the reason? I thought you were drooling over my ass in this skirt." Lizzie accepted his help out of the car, smoothing out her burgundy corduroy skirt.

"Trust me, princess. Your ass in that skirt is giving me a whole different reaction," he whispered against her lips. He kissed her, a groan leaving him as soon as he got a taste of her tongue. If he wasn't careful, he was going to end up walking into the house with a very hard—

"Y'all stop all that nasty shit and get my grandbaby out of the car and into the house! He does not need to be watching y'all getting ready to make him a big brother!"

Lizzie giggled as she pulled away. "Mommy, please! We weren't even doing anything."

"Mhmm, y'all were doing just enough for someone to call the HOA on me. And by someone, I mean that nosy ass Grace Halloway next door." Delilah's voice rose as she said, "I know that nosey heffa is the one that snitched on me and Percy last week when we were out back getting busy in the pergola. Just mad 'cause ain't nobody trying to break her off with a lil' some-thin' somethin'."

"Mommy!" Lizzie shrieked while Alonzo tried not to laugh as he covered Christian's ears. Of course, his son would choose that exact moment to get out of the car.

"Girl, stop all that hollering," Delilah said as she rolled her eyes and went into the house.

"I swear she will never stop being one of the wildest people I know," Alonzo chuckled as they made their way up the drive and into the house.

"She's only gotten worse since she and Percy got married. It's ridiculous!"

"Who's ridiculous?" Kendall asked, walking into the foyer, two of her three kids barreling through the hall right behind her.

She scolded them and yelled something about not saving them when their GG went upside their behinds.

"Your mother got a little loud and wild on the front porch telling a story," Alonzo explained as he pulled his sister-in-law in for a hug.

She relaxed against him, and he could feel her shake her head. "Not her going off about Ms. Halloway again. I told her to let that go. She had no business being nasty out there in the first place. She's too old for that."

"Kennie, please. You're never too old to buss it down, especially in your own backyard." That statement had, of course, come from Makayla.

"Don't encourage her, M&M. She'll only get worse if you do," Lizzie scolded her sister.

"Don't tell me you and Lonzo have never gotten busy somewhere you had no business."

Considering the amount of action his office desk had seen since they'd gotten together, it was no surprise to him that Lizzie actively avoided his eyes and the statement itself by telling Christian to go find his cousins.

"Mhmm, that's what I thought," Makayla snickered.

Leaving the sisters to their teasing, Alonzo gave his wife a quick kiss on the forehead before making his way to the den, where he knew the men of the family would be watching football since it was an Oakwood Stallions game day. Sure enough, Percy, Greg, and Reggie were all seated in various spots as the home team ran a defensive play on the field.

"Gentlemen," Alonzo said, greeting each man with a quick hand grip.

"Good to see you, old man. Rescue me from all this young blood in here," Percy joked. Alonzo was used to the digs at his age. Considering he was ten years Lizzie's senior, it was expected, but he knew it was all in good fun.

"I don't know, Percy, they not looking all that young these

days. In fact, I think they're climbing the age ladder quicker than we are."

"You wish," snorted Greg. Alonzo took a look at the man and was pleased to see that he looked to be in much better spirits than he had at the cigar lounge. He hoped that meant things were going better at home.

Alonzo settled in and watched the game, engaging in friendly debates about which teams would make it through the playoffs and into the conference championship. They must've been talking longer than he realized because before he knew it, Delilah was peeking in, telling them to get washed up for dinner.

"Alonzo, can you help me set the table?" she asked sweetly.

He agreed and found himself chuckling as Percy stood and clapped him on the back. "You know what that means, don't you?"

He nodded. If Delilah was specifically asking someone to "help her set the table," that meant she wanted to get them alone to talk. He had an inkling what this conversation was going to be about and quickly went to wash his hands so he wouldn't keep her waiting for too long.

They worked in silence for a few moments, gathering the dishes out of the china cabinet before he felt her eyes finally settle on him.

"So…from what I understand, that knucklehead lil' boy has finally decided to show his raggedy ass face."

His mother-in-law really was something else. "Apparently so," he said, meeting her eyes.

She kissed her teeth. "I don't know what he wants after all this time. Showing up like he runs the place when all he ever really did was run his mouth." She shook her head. "I have never been an advocate of keeping children away from their parents as long as they aren't a danger to them, but that boy has always tested my patience." She paused, hands falling to her hips. "But I guess I don't get much say in whether or not he gets to meet my grandbaby, do I?"

"With all due respect, Ma? No. That's a decision made between Christian, Lizzie, and myself."

She smirked. "Yeah, that's what that knotty-headed child of mine said, too," she said with a laugh. "At least y'all are on the same page. It'll make it that much easier to put your foot down and protect each other. Just don't forget one thing, Lonzo, baby." He looked at her intently. "That's your little boy in there. Your little boy and my whole heart. So you protect him with everything you've got." She walked over and gave him a pat on the cheek. "And show his sperm donor how a real man takes care of business."

CHAPTER 15

Lizzie

Lizzie was one hundred percent certain she was more nervous about seeing King than Christian was. He'd been talking about it non-stop since she'd let him know that they'd be meeting King on Tuesday after school at his favorite playground. The playground made the most sense out of the list Christian had given her when she asked what things he wanted to do. It also had the added benefits of being both a central location and somewhere that had plenty for him to do if King decided to bail at the last minute. God, she hoped it wouldn't come to that.

Thanks to her flexible schedule, she'd been able to block off her afternoon and only see clients in the morning. Combine that with the blessing that was Christian's early release from school, and they'd been left with plenty of time to get to the park by two o'clock. Alonzo had offered to clear his schedule as well, but Lizzie figured it would be better if today wasn't the day that King met both his son and her husband for the first time. The last thing she needed was for him to show his ass and focus on Alonzo when today was supposed to be all about Christian.

When she noticed Christian running toward her from the jungle gym for the fourth time, she already knew what he was going to ask her before the words left him. "What time is he coming, Mommy?"

Bending down to pull up the zipper on his coat, she sent up a silent thank you that it wasn't too cold today. "He should be here soon. Pull that hat over those ears, please."

Instead of doing as she asked, he kicked his feet at the ground. "Umm…mommy?"

"Yes, baby?"

"If you're mommy and daddy is daddy, then…what am I supposed to call him?"

It was a sensible question, and thanks to all of her other worries trying to suffocate her, it was also one that she hadn't spent much time thinking about. "Well, that's up to you. Do you want to call him dad?" Her stomach twisted at the simple suggestion, but she knew she had to give him the option and let him know that was okay. During their conversations leading up to today, he'd mostly been calling King by his name, but maybe knowing they were going to actually meet made it different for him.

After a beat, Christian shook his head. Lizzie should've been ashamed of the way her stomach unclenched, but she wasn't. She knew he might change his mind at some point, but she'd cross that bridge when they got there.

"Well, that's okay. You can call him Mr. King or Mr. Holden." She gave him a mischievous smile. "Maybe Mr. Lollipop Head if he lets you." That got the result she wanted. He laughed, one of her favorite sounds in the entire world.

"Now, pull your hat down over those ears and go play."

He nodded, adjusted his hat, and took off back to where he'd been playing before. Looking down at her phone, Lizzie tried to tamp down her annoyance. Maybe agreeing to this had been a bad idea after all.

"Damn, and here I was, thinking I might actually beat you here this time."

Had she managed to conjure him up with just her thoughts? As if she'd actually willed him to appear, King stood in front of her, a bouquet of flowers in one hand and a stuffed dragon in the other. Her eyes briefly flickered between both before returning to his face. "Hard to beat us here when, once again, you're late. By almost thirty minutes this time."

He gave her that smile that she'd once loved, but she paid it no mind. He tried to remain unfazed as he handed her the bouquet. "Well, hopefully, these make up for that." She took them begrudgingly but didn't thank him.

Instead, she brought his attention to where it needed to be. "I'll let you give him that dragon yourself."

"I had to take a guess on what to bring. Figured I shouldn't show up empty-handed, but I wasn't sure what he was into, and honestly, I didn't really know how to ask." It wasn't until she noticed the slightly embarrassed look on his face and the way he rubbed the back of his neck that Lizzie realized just how nervous King was. As much as he may irritate the hell out of her, she had to admit that it was sort of…endearing.

Her empty hand grazed his. "Hey, you did good. Honestly. I have a sneaking suspicion he'd like anything you gave him, but it probably doesn't hurt that he's going through a dinosaur phase right now. That's all a dragon is, right? A dinosaur with wings." She gave him a smile, the first one in a long time. "So far, you've got pretty good instincts."

Movement behind him caught her attention and let her know that Christian had noticed them. They had thirty seconds at most before he made his way over. "He's headed this way. Just take a few deep breaths and relax. Be yourself." She thought better of what she said. "The actual charming side of yourself. Not the side that's an asshole."

She didn't have time to pay attention to his reaction because a few seconds later, a little body came barreling into her legs. "Woah there, Mr. Speed Racer! What are you trying to do, knock mommy on her butt?"

"Mommyyy," Christian said, drawing out her title with a smile on his face. "Stop being silly!"

"I'm just saying, any faster, and we'll have to sign you up for the Indy 500!" That sent Christian into a full fit of giggles. She smiled at him before looking toward King. Turning the little boy around so that they were all face-to-face, she made the introductions. "Christian, this is King. King, this is our son…Christian."

It was awkward at first. King obviously didn't know what to do and completely forgot to hand over the stuffed dragon until Christian reached out for it. After a little prodding, the tension finally left King's shoulders. Once he loosened up, so did Christian, which was obvious by the way he dragged him across the playground to show him his favorite set of swings. Lizzie had to admit that watching the two of them together didn't pain her as much as she'd thought it would. It didn't make her uncomfortable, irritable, jealous, or any of the other feelings she'd been worried would show their ugly head. Instead, all she felt was…content. This whole thing wouldn't be easy, and her worries certainly weren't going to disappear overnight, but watching the smile on Christian's face as King chased him across the playground made her feel like all of this would turn out okay.

By the time she got up to join them, tackling the slides and the jungle gym before helping King tackle Christian, just over two hours had gone by. She'd spent the last fifteen minutes smiling non-stop as she watched Christian explain to King why the race car he'd painted at school was "one hundred million times better" than the one his friend Damien made.

"And he didn't even add a white stripe! He just left the whole thing blue even though I told him that white stripes make all race cars faster." The way her child let go of an exasperated sigh and shook his head had her shaking her own in disbelief. He had such a big personality.

"I hate to break up this party and spoil all the fun, but we have to head home," Lizzie called out from her seat on the bench.

"But moooom," Christian started to whine, but Lizzie sent him a look that quickly nipped that in the bud.

"No buts except your little one saying goodbye and heading to the car with me." Christian didn't whine this time, but the pout he liked to pull out to get his way appeared in full force. "Nice try," she said with a smirk. "Put the lip away."

"I mean, if he's not ready to head out yet..." King said, his hands slipping into his pockets.

She turned to look at him. "Don't you start either."

"I'm just saying, what's the harm in staying out here a little while longer? I don't see what the point in rushing home is."

"It's already a quarter till five, and the sun is just about gone. He has homework to do, a bath to take, and dinner to eat." Christian groaned, which drew her eyes down to him. "Which daddy is probably getting ready to start making right now, so..." Her eyes landed back on King, who'd tensed up in the last few seconds. "We have to go."

"Right. Wouldn't want to keep *daddy* waiting," he grumbled.

So that's why he was giving her pushback. Because of Alonzo. Got it. No way in hell was she about to engage with *that*.

"Can King come?" God, she loved him, but sometimes her baby boy had the worst timing. "Can he, mommy? King can come home for dinner and meet daddy, right?"

"Mr. King," she said, avoiding the question.

"He said that I could just call him King, no mister." No way could Lizzie ignore how cute he was standing there staring up at her, his face looking oh so serious.

"He's right, I did. Not many choices since daddy seems to be taken, and I've never been much for being called mister." There was that tick in his jaw again. Yep, he was definitely annoyed. Oh, well.

"Mommy?"

"No," Lizzie sighed. "No, sweetie, King can't come over for dinner. He has other plans this time."

Christian looked ready to ask again, but this time, it was King who answered. Stooping down so they were eye-to-eye, he said, "She's right, little man. I've got to get going, too."

It was clear that he was still a bit upset, but at least he put the lip away. "What about later? Can you come over another day? I can ask daddy and—"

"Sure, little man. Whatever you want," King said, cutting him off before Lizzie had the chance.

He can't be serious.

Having King in her house had not been part of the plan. Maybe eventually, but certainly not this early in the game. Then again, wrecking plans was exactly what King had a knack for.

"Sure," she responded through gritted teeth. "Now say good-bye, Christian."

"Bye, King!" The joy in his voice was so obvious that Lizzie almost forgot to be irritated.

"Bye, little man. I'll see you next time, okay?"

The two shared a hug before King turned to Lizzie with his arms outstretched. "Figured since I'm handing out hugs, you might want one, too."

Her nose wrinkled in disgust. "I'm good."

Lizzie took Christian's hand in her own and led him back to the car. After making sure he was strapped in, they made their way home while Christian spent the entire ride recounting every-thing that he'd done with King as if she hadn't been there to witness them firsthand. She knew it would be more of the same once they got home and he had a chance to see Alonzo. If nothing else, at least she could say that today had been a success. Even if it did have a *Guess Who's Coming to Dinner* ending.

No way in hell. There's no way his ass is setting foot in my damn house.

Allowing King to get to know Christian was one thing, but inviting him into her private space? Into the home that she and Alonzo had built together? The idea was nerve-wracking. Then there was the matter of explaining that to her husband.

Oh, by the way! You know my deadbeat baby daddy? The one who popped up out of thin air? Yeah, he's trying to come over and hang out for a while. You don't mind, do you?

Alonzo may be one of the most understanding people she'd ever met in her life, but everyone had their limits, and this just might be his.

After pulling into the garage, Christian burst through the door and into the house. It was pointless telling him to slow down because, by the time she tried to, he was already gone. Whether intentionally or unintentionally, Lizzie took her time gathering their things and following him inside. Of course, her penchant for perfect timing meant that she entered the house and made her way to the kitchen at the exact moment that Christian was telling Alonzo about the dinner invitation.

"And he's going to come to our house to eat dinner, daddy! Mommy said he couldn't come today even though I really wanted him to, but that's okay because I know when he does come, you're going to make something really, really good."

One of Alonzo's eyebrows created a perfect arch. "Dinner?" He looked over at Lizzie, who could do nothing but shrug her shoulders. "Hmmm. Well, it sounds like you had a busy day. Why don't you go wash your hands and then grab your homework out of your bookbag? You can do it in the living room while I finish working on dinner."

"But I—"

"Homework," Alonzo said sternly.

Christian quickly went to do as he asked, leaving the two of them in the kitchen on their own.

"No kisses today?"

Despite her mood, Lizzie felt the corner of her mouth lift in a smile. There was no other encouragement needed for her to go over and wrap her arms around his waist. Leaning up and meeting him halfway, she placed a lingering kiss on his lips before her face fell against his chest. She closed her eyes at the feel of him pressing a kiss to the top of her head.

"Rough day?" he asked, doing his best to stir the spaghetti sauce in the pan without jostling her too much.

"Not particularly. It actually went a lot better than I thought it would."

"That's what happens when everyone is on their best behavior," he chuckled.

"Yeah, well, I wish your child had been on his best behavior instead of opening his mouth and inviting that man to our house."

This time, Alonzo unwrapped her arms and took a few steps away. As irrational as it was, the gesture irritated her a bit. Without the safety of his arms, she felt exposed. Was he really just doing what he needed to do for cooking, or was he stepping away from her?

"About that, what exactly did you say to Christian about this whole…dinner invite?"

"I told him sure."

"And you're okay with that? You really think it's a good idea?"

"No, but I had to say something. Once Christian said that, I was just ready to get the hell out of there. What did you want me to say, no?"

With a shake of his head, he brought over the box of uncooked pasta that he'd gone to grab. "No, but it would've been nice if you'd told him we'd talk about it first. That's not exactly a one-person decision."

"Well, my intention was to talk to you about it after dinner, but clearly, you'd rather get into this now."

The sigh he let out as he rested his hands and the box on the counter made it clear that he was feeling a bit exasperated. "I'm not trying to *get into* anything right now, Lizzie. I'm just—"

"Just questioning my decision, right?" Her irritation grew the longer this conversation carried on. Logically, she knew she was taking something out on Alonzo that really had nothing to do with him, but she couldn't stop herself. Before she set foot in the house, she'd been trying to come up with ways to get out of the invitation, and now here she was, practically defending it. "Christian invited him. This isn't something you just get to shut down!"

"That's not what I'm doing!" Alonzo rarely raised his voice, and as soon as he did, both of their gazes looked in the direction of the living room. When it was clear that Christian wasn't going to come and see what the noise was about, Lizzie focused back on Alonzo. The hurt look in his eyes struck her right in the chest. "Don't do this, princess. You asked me to be an active participant, so that's what I'm trying to do."

And she knew that, she did. Still, that didn't stop her from crossing her arms to look everywhere but at him as she said, "I'm going to take a shower before dinner. We can finish talking about this later."

CHAPTER 16

Alonzo

After his wife had walked away in the middle of their discussion, Alonzo knew that shit could go downhill and fast if he wasn't careful. So, after a painfully silent dinner and a pillow talk session with an extremely awkward start, he'd suggested going to see Dr. Brunson together for her next session. That was how the two of them ended up together in the therapist's office just a couple of days later.

"Alonzo, it's good to see you again. I know it's been a little while since you joined us for a session."

He chuckled. "Yeah, it has. Thank you for letting me crash your time today." His gaze traveled to Lizzie before settling back on Dr. Brunson.

"I would say you're welcome, but I think there's someone else here that has more control over that than I do."

Nodding in agreement, he repositioned himself so that he was facing his wife instead. "Thank you, Lizzie. I appreciate you agreeing to let me come with you today."

He watched as a few emotions crossed her eyes before she answered, "Thank you for suggesting it."

Alonzo hadn't even realized he'd been holding his breath until she said that. Even though they'd been functioning as normal over the last day or so, there still seemed to be a cloud hanging over them. One that neither of them wanted to acknowledge for fear of upsetting the other.

"Would you like to tell me what brought this on?"

With a weak smile, Lizzie said, "I'm pretty sure you already know the answer to that, Kiera."

"Maybe so, but we both know I don't like to make assumptions or guesses." That was certainly something he remembered from the few sessions that he'd met with both women. "Alonzo, why don't you start us off?"

With one more look at Lizzie, he turned back toward Dr. Brunson. "Things have been...I suppose you could call it tense." She gestured for him to continue. "I know Lizzie's spoken with you about the fact that Christian's biological dad has come back into the picture wanting to get to know him."

"She has. Is that what has you all off balance? I'm sure it's a big adjustment making room for someone in your life. Certainly even more so when it's unexpected."

"No, it's not necessarily that. I wasn't exactly happy that King showed up out of nowhere, but I also didn't have any intention of adding to the stress I knew his reappearance was already causing Lizzie. I let Lizzie know from the beginning that I would support whatever she decided to do."

"But..."

"I don't know if there's really a 'but' involved. Lizzie and I both agreed that Christian had the right to meet and develop a relationship with King as long as no boundaries were overstepped and it wouldn't hurt him."

"So, is that the issue? Do you feel like some boundaries have been overstepped?"

Alonzo hesitated, unsure of how he should answer. He didn't want to hurt Lizzie, but he also wanted to be truthful. That was why they were here, right? "I wouldn't say that, no. The two of them met, and from what I understand, everything went fine, but when it was all said and done, Christian invited King to dinner."

"And that's what you have a problem with?"

"No, his problem stems from the fact that I didn't shut the invitation down when it happened," Lizzie said, entering the conversation.

"No," he responded, shaking his head. "That's not what I was trying to say."

"Well, that's what it sounded like! You made it seem like you had a problem with the prospect of King coming to dinner even though it was clearly something Christian wanted."

"I understand that, Lizzie, and I'm not disputing it. Like I said before, my issue isn't with the fact that Christian invited him. He was excited after having a great time. It just would've been nice if, in that moment, you would have pumped the brakes on it just a bit and let King know that it was something that needed to be discussed."

"So, what, because I didn't do it exactly how you would've wanted me to, it's a problem?"

"No, the problem is that when I tried to talk to you about it, you immediately shut me out! You didn't even make an attempt to hear what I was trying to tell you, and suddenly, it was a problem that I wanted to have some input on what was happening after you made a point to tell me not to be passive about this situation or my feelings. It's like you're punishing me for trying to be honest."

Even he could hear the strain in his voice. It hurt him to his core to think that the united front they were supposed to have could possibly crash so quickly.

"Is that what you're trying to do, Lizzie? Punish Alonzo for speaking up?" It gave him a little relief when she shook her head. "Okay. What was it that he did or said wrong? Tell him."

Watching her pull her bottom lip between her teeth as her

eyes began to water damn near broke Alonzo's heart. He hated that he was causing her so much pain and frustration, but he honestly didn't understand where things had gone left.

"I don't even think it was about you at that moment." She moved closer to him, leaning across her chair to take his hand in hers. "Honestly, I don't even want King to come for dinner. It feels too soon, especially if it's already causing this sort of chaos. And I had every intention of saying that or something that would at least put a pause in the conversation, but King cut me off before I could."

Of course, he did. Based on what he knew about him, it wasn't hard to imagine that King had purposely jumped on the opportunity Christian had given him before Lizzie could object.

"Once that happened, I was just ready to get the hell out of there."

"So you were already aggravated?" Dr. Brunson said, nodding as if she understood.

"Definitely. The whole way home, all I could think about was how King had managed to weasel his way into our damn house. He hasn't been back but a hot minute, and he's already trying to cause chaos. My emotions were already all over the place, so when I walked through the door, and you started asking questions…"

"You immediately went on the defensive because your walls were already up," Alonzo finished for her.

"Yeah," she answered, her voice close to a whisper. "And I'm sorry about that. I shouldn't have jumped down your throat for wanting to have a conversation."

"No, you shouldn't have, but I also should've given you a moment to breathe before starting in on the questions. I knew you were already a bit antsy about him meeting Christian, so it makes sense that you were feeling some type of way afterward as well. I'm sorry I didn't give you time to process."

Staring into her eyes, he could already feel the cloud disappearing. The truth was they were both in uncharted territory. Dr. Brunson said as much.

"You both have to be willing to give each other a bit of grace. This is a situation that neither one of you thought that you would find yourselves in, so it's going to take a bit of patience navigating the waters. In the meantime, you just have to remember to keep the lines of communication open. I don't think anyone is wrong in this situation, not even King."

That caused both of their heads to snap back a bit.

"Yes, shocking, I know. But you're both assuming that King had ill intentions, and you know what, maybe some part of him did hope that jumping in would cause a bit of strife, but there's also a possibility that he just didn't want the opportunity to spend more time with Christian pass him by. If he thought Lizzie was going to say no, he may have decided that was the best way to get what he wanted. I'm not saying that he was right for that; I'm just suggesting maybe his intentions weren't malicious. The only person who really knows for sure is King himself."

Alonzo understood the point that the doctor was trying to convey, but if he were a betting man, he'd say that even if a part of King didn't want to miss out on the opportunity to spend more time with Christian, he also just didn't want to give Lizzie a chance to think too much about it.

"The question is, now that you both understand where the other was coming from, how are you going to handle the situation?"

As much as he hated to admit it, Alonzo knew what needed to happen. "I think we should let him come over."

"What?" Lizzie's face was in complete disbelief. If the situation wasn't mildly serious, he would've laughed at her expression.

"This is clearly something that Christian really wants. He's mentioned it a few times, asking when it can happen."

"Yeah, but that doesn't mean it has to happen now!"

"What better time than now? Other than a bit of discomfort

on our part, there's no real reason that we shouldn't just rip the Band-Aid off and give it a try."

A soft chuckle came from Dr. Brunson's direction, and it brought a smile to Alonzo's face. "I'm going to have to meet him at some point, right? Better to do it now than put it off until later. And no, this isn't just because of Christian. I want to be able to meet him so that he understands getting to know my son means getting to know me too. And I want him to know that early on because maybe it'll help us avoid problems down the line." It was wishful thinking, to say the least. "But if you're not comfortable with that, I won't push. I meant it when I said that I don't want to add to your stress or make things worse. We're partners in this, so if you want to pump the brakes, then we'll pump them."

Her answer didn't come right away, but when it did, it was definitive. "Okay. Let's do it. I'll call King and set it up for this weekend."

CHAPTER 17

Lizzie

"I don't know what shit you're over there smokin', but you need to throw it out immediately."

If Lizzie rolled her eyes any harder, they would get stuck in her head. She'd been listening to Makayla bitch and moan for the last twenty minutes about King coming over for dinner. The way she was talking, one might've thought that Makayla was the one about to have dinner with her damn baby daddy.

"No one over here is under the influence, M&M." Though that would probably make this shit a lot easier. "We just decided that if this is something that's going to make Christian happy, then we need to try and make the best of the situation. If King is actually going to make an effort to be in his life, that's not something that Lonzo or I want to stand in the way of."

"That's all well and good, Lizzie. Me, myself, and I would have told that nigga to kick rocks and kiss my Black ass. But why, pray tell, does this little family dinner have to take place in your home? Y'all can't meet that man in a restaurant or something? Take his ass to Applebee's."

"First of all, you know I can't stand their food," Lizzie giggled. "Second, yes, we could have met him somewhere in public. Honestly, I suggested that, but Alonzo insisted on King coming here." She still wasn't sure what her husband was thinking, inviting that man into their personal space, but after spending the rest of the session with her therapist trying to work out the details, she finally agreed.

"Hmmm…home court advantage? Okay, my brother-in-love might just be onto something." A low voice said something in the background, and Makayla let out a giggle. "Okay, I gotta get ready to go. Reggie and I are meeting Avery and Lucas for pool, but real quick, have you talked to Kendall today?"

Lizzie felt her mood dip just a bit. "Not really. I sent her a text earlier checking in, but other than her sending me a thumbs up, she didn't have much of a response." The silence that came from her sister's end of the line spoke volumes. "What happened?"

After a brief moment of hesitation, Makayla said, "So, this is just hearsay for right now, but Reggie let it slip earlier that Greg said something about moving out."

Her body's reaction was immediate. She felt her heart skip a beat, and the muscles in her hand tightened. Knowing that Kendall was struggling so much made Lizzie sick.

"Listen, don't worry about it now, but I think once you get through this dinner and we get through your anniversary party, we're going to need to have a serious sister heart-to-heart."

"Agreed."

Reggie made another comment in the background, and after huffing and puffing like the big bad wolf, Makayla let Lizzie know she had to go, and the two quickly ended the call.

Now that she had time to herself, it was hard for Lizzie's mind not to wander toward the night's plan. Alonzo assured her that he would take care of dinner, firing up his grill despite the fact that it was near the end of January. It didn't matter what month or season it was, her husband was always ready to throw something on the grill. Tonight, he would be cooking up some steaks along with peppers, onions, and asparagus. There were twice-baked potatoes already in the oven, and Christian had been adamant about baking snickerdoodle cookies at his grandmother's house on Friday specifically so that everyone could have them for dessert tonight. That left her with nothing to do except… worry the shit out of herself.

She tried not to think of all the things that could go wrong tonight, but it wasn't easy. When the echo of the doorbell sounded throughout the house, reality smacked her in the face, and she suddenly found herself wishing that she'd canceled.

With a quick prayer and a deep breath, Lizzie made her way out of her bedroom and down the hallway, smoothing down the front of her oversized bronze turtleneck, ready to answer the door. Based on the fact that she could hear King's voice echoing through the foyer, it was clear that someone had beaten her to it.

The sight of the love of her life standing in front of her ex, chuckling and offering a friendly handshake, was surreal. Was this the Twilight Zone?

"Mommy, look, look! King is here!" Despite her reservations about the night, seeing her son's face light up was enough to make her heart burst.

"Mhmm, I see," she said, unable to contain the laugh that followed. Christian was practically bouncing on the balls of his feet.

Her eyes traveled back to King, who was looking at her in a way that…well, let's just say it probably wasn't the most appropriate look. If Alonzo noticed, he didn't let on, just accepted her body as she walked up and pressed her side into his before placing a kiss against her temple.

"King." She wondered if she'd actually managed to give the smile she'd been attempting or if it'd come out more as a grimace.

"Bug," he said, a smile of his own appearing as his eyes gave her a once-over. "Looking good, as always."

This nigga. "Thank you," she responded, keeping it simple.

"My auntie always told me not to show up to people's houses empty-handed, so I figured another bouquet of flowers was probably a good look." As the words left his lips, he handed her the flowers in question.

"Look! I got a basketball, Mommy!" Sure enough, she noticed that Christian was holding a ball almost bigger than him.

"How nice."

"Well, since little man told me about the school team, I figured he should have one at home to practice with. Maybe one he and I can shoot around. You know, show him some of the family skills and whatnot."

It took everything in her not to point out that he already had one or two basketballs around the house. She didn't want to be antagonistic, and the important thing was that King had brought his son something in an attempt to bond with him. It was at least a step in the right direction. One that gave her a bit of hope.

That feeling quickly disappeared once he added, "I would've brought something for you, big dog, but I figured ain't no need for that, I'm sure."

Lizzie felt Alonzo give her side a pinch, probably to keep her from responding. "Nah, you're right. I've already got everything I need right here." That brought a genuine smile to her face. "Like I was saying before this beautiful woman joined us, you have perfect timing. I just pulled the steaks off the grill."

"Bet."

"Monster, how about you go put the ball away, show King here your room, and then let him help you wash up for dinner?"

"Okay, daddy."

"Baby, you good to help me set the table?"

"Of course," Lizzie smiled before placing a quick peck on Alonzo's lips.

The two pairs went their separate ways, and Lizzie took the opportunity to take a breath and get herself together.

"Princess, you've got to relax," Alonzo said, taking the flowers from her and grabbing a vase. The one she would typically use was already occupied by the gladiolas that he bought her every week, but they had a spare one around the kitchen somewhere.

"I am relaxed!"

"Not according to that grimace you shot him at the door." His deep chuckle made her kiss her teeth, but she couldn't help the small smile it drew from her as well.

"I'm just a little off, okay!" She shook her head as she quickly washed her hands and grabbed the plates for the dining room table while Alonzo put everything on serving platters. "This is just weird all the way around. What about you? Are you okay?"

"Just fine." She shot him an inquisitive look. "I promise, princess. Listen, I already told you that this whole thing was fine with me. I just want what's best for Christian. Besides, ain't no way I'm gonna let another nigga setting foot in my house throw me off my shit or have me worried. I'm too grown for that."

"Good to know," King responded as he entered the kitchen, even though the statement wasn't directed toward him. "I can respect that."

Alonzo shrugged. "Just speaking the truth."

Slightly annoyed that King had been listening to their conversation, Lizzie narrowed her eyes. "Where's Christian?"

"Oh, he's coming. He had to handle his business, so I wanted to give him some privacy and whatnot." He took a look at his flowers, now sitting on the kitchen counter. "You like the flowers? I remember daisies being your favorite."

"Gladiolas are my favorite." She tried to keep her tone light, but it came out clipped anyway because, of course, he didn't remember that.

"Since when?"

"Since always."

"Nah, that's not how I remember things."

"Well, that doesn't surprise me, King, but that doesn't change the fact that it's true. I told you that more than once years ago, but *you* never really caught on." To be fair, he'd rarely bought her flowers anyway, but whenever he did, it was usually daisies. She'd stopped complaining after a while because she was just happy to be getting anything from him. It was the thought that counted, but damn, did she love the fact that it had only taken one mention of her actual favorites to Alonzo before they started dating for him to commit the fact to memory and behave accordingly. "But they're beautiful all the same, so thank you."

Tick. Tick. Tick. There went that jaw again.

Thankfully, Christian came bouncing into the kitchen, breaking up the tension as he led King to the dining room. Alonzo shot her a wink before following with some of the food. After making quick work of setting the table and taking their seats, with Christian sitting next to King and Alonzo and Lizzie sitting across from them, the group dug into dinner. It was pretty easy to let the baby of the quartet dominate the conversation. As he hadn't seen the other man since Tuesday and had only spoken to him one other time since, Christian made a point to update him on every little detail that had occurred during their time apart.

When he finally took a breath, King turned to Alonzo. "So, what exactly is it that you do? I meant to ask Bug here, but you know…we didn't really get around to talking about you much."

Lizzie could've chalked his statement up to something innocent, but the smirk he sent her way was anything but.

"I run my own financial analyst company. I've always worked in finance but finally decided that I wanted to not only work for myself but work to help other Black people and people of color. Do what I can to give back."

"Daddy teaches classes, too," Christian added, not wanting to be left out of the conversation.

"Is that so?"

"Yep. That's actually how we met," Lizzie said. Alonzo sent a wink in her direction, and she rolled her eyes, though her smile was bright as ever.

"Scoping out the hot young student, huh?"

King's comment was definitely a bit of shade, but Alonzo seemed to take it in stride. "I wouldn't say all that, but Lizzie definitely caught my eye early on."

"Not a surprise. She's always been a beautiful woman."

She knew King was trying to send her a compliment but silently wished he'd kept it to himself.

"I won't argue with you there, but it was more than that. I don't think anyone could deny just how magnetic her attitude and drive was? From the moment she set foot in that classroom, she made it clear that she had a goal to achieve for her and Christian. I just wanted to do what I could to be part of that."

Lizzie was sure she couldn't love this man any more than she did right now. She never got tired of hearing him tell his side of the story.

Looking at Christian, Alonzo added, "And this little monster right here? He probably stole my heart even quicker than his mama did." The silly face that Alonzo pulled got a flurry of giggles out of Christian.

"Daddy! That's not a good silly face at all."

"I guess I'll have to try harder next time," Alonzo laughed.

The moment was adorable. So adorable, in fact, that King took it upon himself to break it up.

"Cute." Based on the way he said it, King thought it was anything but. "I gotta say, though, if someone would've told me back in the day that Bug would have decided to go for a nerd, especially one your age, I would've for sure thought they were lying." He paused a little too long for the "No offense" that followed to be genuine.

"None taken. If being good with money and being able to

provide for my family and community makes me a nerd, well, then I guess that's just what it is. I honestly look at it as using my talents to be the type of man I can be proud of."

"I mean, I guess, but I could never see myself all buttoned up, tie on, and sitting at a desk all day, every day. That's for damn sure. Nah, I like my freedom too much."

"Don't we know it," Lizzie mumbled before she could think twice.

After a few awkward moments, Christian jumped in again. "Why do you call mommy Bug?" With his face scrunched up the way it was, he practically looked like her twin, something Alonzo loved to point out.

"Well, your mommy and I have known each other a long time, and when you have a bond like the one we have—"

"Had," Lizzie quickly amended.

"Riiight. Like the one we *had*, you get to create lots of different memories. I started calling her Bug after our second date. I picked her up so that we could go play mini golf. I was driving my motorcycle at the time, and let me tell you something, your mama looked good on the back of my bike." King's eyes drifted toward Lizzie, and the intensity of his gaze made her focus on her plate. "Real good."

After a brief pause, Alonzo cleared his throat. "I can imagine."

"So anyway, the entire time we're there, it was like every bug in the place was drawn to her. I guess they thought she was just as beautiful as I did. It got so bad at one point that as she was trying to swat them away, she tripped over her own feet, screamed, and fell into the pond."

Lizzie groaned. "It was so embarrassing."

"Yeah, but it was definitely a date we'll never forget." His eyes found Christian, and he finished by saying, "And so, since those bugs gave me one of my favorite memories of your mom, I've been calling her that ever since."

As the conversation picked back up, this time turning toward Christian's own experience with creepy crawlers, Lizzie allowed her mind to drift. She remembered that day just as King described it. For once, he hadn't changed or embellished any part. She'd been so giddy about going out with him and wanted everything to be perfect. When she'd taken that fall, she'd have bet money that he'd never call her again, but instead, they both just managed to spend the next twenty minutes laughing as she tried to dry off and fix her hair. At the time, she'd loved the nickname and the story. Now, though, it was just a reminder of how great things were before King started to show his true colors.

Lizzie tuned back in just as Alonzo was asking him another question. "So, what have you been up to the last few years? Anything interesting?"

"I moved around a bit, trying to see what worked for me. I've been doing security for a while now, and it's not bad. It lets me meet new people, see new places. I'm starting to think that there's nothing like home, though." His eyes settled back on Lizzie. "Started thinking it was time to come back home and maybe set up shop here. Pick up a few things where they left off." Lizzie could take a wild guess on what those things might be, but she wasn't interested.

"Well, I'm sure Morgan will be happy to hear that. I know she's missed having you around Oakwood," she said, giving him a small smile.

"Yeah, well, I'm hoping that she's not the only one."

The silence that settled over the table was heavy. Had he really just said that? King always had some audacity, but to sit up here and try to disrespect their household so blatantly? He was out of pocket, and he clearly wasn't finished. "It's about time I step up on my grown man shit and all that. Settle some things and make my presence known." His eyes found their way back to Alonzo, who only chuckled.

"Well, I'm happy to hear it. As someone who's already a

grown man, let me know if you need a few pointers. I'm sure you could use the assist."

———

"Have I mentioned that you are literally the most patient person I know?"

Lizzie and Alonzo had settled in on the couch in the family room. A rerun of their favorite medical drama was playing on the television, though they weren't giving it too much of their attention. With dinner officially over two hours ago and King long gone, the dishes washed, and Christian tucked into bed for the night, Lizzie could admit that she was bone-tired.

Alonzo gave her a look as she sipped her glass of wine. "Considering your family, that's not really saying much. Besides, I'm pretty sure that award actually goes to you."

"First of all, don't come for my family like that. Their raggedy asses belong to you just like they belong to me." He immediately let out a booming laugh, and it brought a smile to her face. "Second, I wasn't including myself in that assessment."

"And so humble, too," he added as he resumed her foot massage.

"The only way I know how to be," she teased. The laugh that was supposed to follow quickly turned into a moan that sounded suspiciously like, "Ooooh, shit," as his fingers chose that exact moment to dig into the ball of her foot.

Lizzie set her glass on the coffee table and shimmied down until she was flat on the couch, her head propped up slightly on a throw pillow. The change in position didn't stop Alonzo from pampering her with his magic fingers. It only encouraged him. His foot rubs were mind-blowing and very close to orgasm-inducing. Her husband was certainly a man of many talents.

"Seriously, though, baby. You really took tonight in stride, and I know King's irritating ass did not make it easy." The snide comments hadn't stopped until after they'd closed the door behind him, but none of them seemed to faze Alonzo too much. She'd been well aware of how laid-back her man was but seeing him not even break a sweat while he handled the situation did something extra to her.

"Honestly, he's all bark and no bite. He wanted to get a rise out of me because he feels like he's got something to prove, and who am I to tell him otherwise? As long as he doesn't get overly disrespectful, he can talk all he wants. It's not doing shit but sounding like Charlie Brown to both you and me. No point in letting it get under my skin."

"I guess," she sighed. "I just wish he didn't get on my nerves so bad. He really thinks he can just walk in and get whatever he wants, including me and Christian."

"Well, we both know that's not true. Besides, I'll never be insecure over another nigga, especially not a young one who can't even come close to playing my role. I've been doing my thing for almost four years. There's nothing he can do to change that."

"You damn right," she said, the irritation she'd been feeling for the better part of the evening finally dissipating at his words. She knew what Alonzo was saying was true. King loved disrupting everyone around him. Despite his best efforts, he hadn't succeeded tonight, and that was all that mattered.

"I can't believe we've been married for three years." She let the tension roll off of her shoulders and closed her eyes, letting the sounds of the tv and the fireplace fill the air.

"I can."

Her foot caught him in the stomach, and she felt a sense of satisfaction at his pained grunt. "Rude."

His chuckle joined the other sounds in the room. "You know I didn't mean it like that, princess. I just meant that I always saw you as my wife. The moment I laid eyes on you, nose scrunched, hair under that baseball cap, teeth nibbling on the side of your pen, the first thing that came to mind was, 'She's my forever.'"

"Baby..." she said, peeking through one eyelid, her tone sickly sweet, "you are so full of shit." They both burst into laughter so loud she worried for a moment that it would wake Christian.

"Okay, so maybe that wasn't my first thought. Or my second. My first thought might've leaned more toward, 'Baby, it's a pen, not a sandwich.'" Lizzie kissed her teeth at that and went in for a kick with the other foot, but he saw it coming this time and caught it in his hand. He placed a kiss on her second toe, the one he always said was his favorite because it was slightly longer than her big one. "But trust me when I say it only took two more sessions for me to realize the only future feasible was one with you in it."

She thought back to the sessions he was referring to. At the time, she'd been hyper-focused on learning everything she could about starting her own business and becoming financially secure. Getting into a relationship, especially with someone ten years her senior, had been the last thing on her mind. She hadn't even been willing to give Alonzo a chance, too sure that he was looking for nothing more than some pretty girl to keep him busy for a night or two. There were plenty of women there who were already more than happy to oblige. In fact, Alonzo's dating life and availability had both been hot topics among the other women in her class.

"I think I asked you out about ten times before you finally said yes."

"It was eleven, but who's counting?" He'd been persistent in his pursuit, and she had to admit it had felt good to have someone show more than a passing interest in her. He'd never pressured her but also didn't shy away from making it known that he had every intention of taking her out, no matter how long it took.

Lizzie sat up and pulled her feet from Alonzo's grip. Switching positions, she placed her head face up in his lap this time, her fingers reaching out to ghost over his beard. He took her hand in his and brought each finger to his lips for a light kiss.

"Lucky number eleven."

Warmth spread through her chest, and she used her fingers to tug on his beard. He understood the gesture immediately and bent down to place a kiss on her lips. The kiss was sweet, just a tinge of heat behind it, but his love for her came through above all else.

"Saying yes was the best decision I ever made," she whispered against his lips.

He touched his forehead to hers. "And asking was mine."

CHAPTER 18

Lizzie

"I love you, baby, but absolutely not." Alonzo chuckled as he held the car door open for her. Sunday had come and gone, and soon, Monday was well on its way to being over as well. After taking Christian to meet King after work for a little fun at the arcade, Lizzie had ventured home, where the two of them had dinner with Alonzo, and then Makayla had come over to spend some time with her nephew so that she and Alonzo could have a quick date night to start their week off the right way. Dr. Brunson had mentioned during their session that it was important for them to find time to connect, both because of King's re-entry into their lives and because of their upcoming anniversary. So, it'd been decided a movie date was very much on the agenda.

"Why not?" Lizzie climbed out of the car and leaned into him as he wrapped his arms around her. "You have no idea how sexy you would look in a bolo tie."

The way he cringed at the mention of what he'd told her he was starting to think of as his arch-nemesis caused her to laugh. They'd been going over anniversary plans on the ride to the movie theater when she'd mentioned the outfits she was putting together for them for the party. He seemed content to let her do her thing, but the minute she mentioned the bolo tie, he'd drawn the line.

"I'm going to win you over. Promise you that," she said, her tone determined.

"Awww, princess, I thought you already knew." His lips grazed hers as he whispered his next words against them. "You won me over a long time ago."

She smiled into the kiss, their bodies melting together, shielding them from the bite of the cold. They forgot where they were for a brief moment, their tongues reacquainting themselves with one another until they heard the snickers of a few innocent bystanders.

"Come on here, woman, before you get me an indecency charge." Alonzo took her hand and led her out of the parking lot toward the movie theater. Lizzie found herself getting excited as they made their way into the lobby to the person responsible for checking tickets. She'd mentioned wanting to see the all-female-led war movie multiple times since first seeing the preview months ago. Luckily, Alonzo had no complaints, eager to see some of his favorite actresses battle it out on screen.

Honestly, after a long day of dealing with clients and then having to see King, sharing an extra-large popcorn with her husband sounded like the perfect night. And thankfully, that wouldn't be all the couple would be sharing since they'd chosen the upscale theater in Oakwood that served standard movie snacks along with alcohol and actual entrées. She could practically feel the wagyu sliders melting on her tongue already.

"I meant to ask earlier, how did things go with King?" They hadn't gotten a chance to talk much about the interaction since Alonzo had been late getting home.

"Ugh, for Christian, it was fine. For me, it took everything I had not to shove a joystick up his ass."

At his raised eyebrows, she shook her head. "Just more of the same comments he was making when he came by for dinner on Saturday. Trying to reminisce about old times, bringing up dates and how video games used to be our thing or whatever." Kissing her teeth, she added, "Which, they were never *our* thing. They were always his thing. What he preferred to do instead of actually spending time with me or having a conversation. But of course, he doesn't remember it that way."

It'd been hard trying to tamp down her annoyance, but she'd done her best because the last thing she wanted was for Christian to witness her going off when he was having such a good time.

"Well, I'm not surprised he's out here trying to rewrite history."

"Neither am I, but I just wish he'd stop trying to take all these walks down memory lane. I'm not interested, but he doesn't seem to understand that."

She knew that King was being willfully ignorant, and it was plucking her last nerve.

"Maybe I should have a talk with him," Alonzo said as they worked to find their seats. Once they sat down, they both picked up the small menu to see if anything other than what they'd already decided on jumped out at them.

"No, it's okay. I can handle it. The last thing we need is him trying to get into another pissing match with you. Now, help me decide between the truffle fries and the onion rings. I'm starving."

Two and a half hours later, Lizzie could officially count date night as a success. Despite Alonzo teasing her about sniffling and tearing up at the death of one of the main characters, she'd had a great time. Even now, as they made their way back to the car, he couldn't seem to help himself as he chuckled again while she swiped at her face and shot him a dirty look.

"I don't see what's so funny."

"Absolutely nothing," he answered, though that didn't stop him from taking one last snicker or two.

"Don't think I didn't catch you over there getting emotional, too."

"I have no idea what you're talking about." Before she could respond, he continued, "I was thinking we could make one more stop before we head home. Grab a bit of dessert for the night."

"Silly me," she teased as she waited for him to open the passenger side door. "I thought *I* was going to be dessert."

The heated look that he gave her set Lizzie on fire, causing her to rub her thighs together for some relief. "Oh, trust me, I plan on cleaning that plate, too." He helped her into the car and quickly made his way to the other side. "But I know how your sweet tooth tends to show up right after mine gets satisfied."

He was right about that. "Promises, promises, baby."

"Well, you know I always keep my promises."

———

"I jus—" The words got stuck in Lizzie's throat as Alonzo's tongue wrapped around her clit, and the feel of the water from the showerhead soaked her back. He hadn't been playing when he said he was going to use her to satisfy his sweet tooth. They'd barely been home ten minutes before he was stripping her naked and pulling her into the standalone shower to have his way with her. The way this man didn't hesitate to drop to his knees and give her exactly what she craved was…otherworldly.

"Use your words, princess," he mumbled. The pounding in her ears as she climbed closer and closer to her peak was so loud that she almost missed what he said. It seemed to drown out everything, including her breathless moans.

"I *caaan't.*" Her words came out as a whine and part of her hated the sound, but there was another side of her that relished in the fact that he could bring something like that out of her.

It was clear that he didn't care about that as the strokes of his tongue became more persistent, causing her thighs to shake. Thank God she was on the marble shower bench; otherwise, her legs would have surely given out.

Her breath came in pants as the trusted feeling rose inside of her. Only a few seconds passed before she moaned his name, and the sound of Alonzo groaning was just the catalyst she needed to go right over the edge.

She knew he would have stayed like that, greedily taking everything she had to give, but she had other plans in mind.

"Baby, stop," she moaned, attempting to push him away.

"But you taste so fucking good," he groaned, pulling away to nibble on her inner thigh before gazing up into her eyes.

"It's my turn to taste you."

She would have laughed at the way he eagerly stood, ready to meet her demands, if it weren't for the rumble she heard in his chest and the heat behind his eyes. There was no encouragement needed, not when his thick shaft was ready and waiting for her. Her hand slid and twisted around him with ease. As a bead of precum appeared, her tongue flicked across it, collecting it the same way she would any reward.

"Do you realize how beautiful you look on your knees, princess?" His words came out on a groan as she took the tip and only the tip of him into her mouth, her tongue gliding across him in search of more salty goodness.

"I want you to tell me," she answered, pulling away just enough to leave light kisses along his dick as she held his gaze with her own.

His throaty, *"Fuck,"* hit Lizzie right between her thighs, and she had to stop herself from dipping her fingers between her legs to find some relief.

Instead, she wrapped her lips around him, taking him deeper and deeper into her throat. She'd taken him halfway down when his hand found the back of her wet hair, his fingers digging into her scalp to hold her there.

"Swallow."

It was a one-word command, but she followed it without hesitation, enjoying the moan it pulled out of him when the motion caused him to slide in even further. Her hands gripped the back of his thighs as she began to bob back and forth, allowing him to reach the back of her throat and enjoying the curses he let fly each time.

"You look like you were made for this."

His praise only made her go harder. She loved the way he tasted, loved how he slid down her throat at the perfect angle, filling her, letting her tongue and mouth swirl around him.

"Should be a *goddamn* crime."

As his words became more strained, his strokes became more forceful, and the way she sucked him became more desperate. She could feel the saliva sliding down her chin, the water pelting her back and sliding over the top of her head. She wasn't sure which was ruining her makeup more, the shower or the tears starting to form in her eyes, but as Alonzo looked down at her and said, "You're making a fucking mess, princess, just the way I like it," she couldn't help but close her eyes and bring her right hand down to relieve the pressure that was starting to build again.

He offered moans and words of encouragement as she touched herself, wanting to find release as she tried to give him his, and before long, a bolt of electricity shot from her clit to the rest of her body as she came against her hand and released whimpers around his dick. She was so lost in the euphoria that Alonzo took over the pace, fucking her mouth until he was coming down her throat as he hissed in pleasure, barely able to watch her swallow every drop.

All she could think was *damn, I love this man.*

It was hours later that a steady buzzing sound broke her

orgasm-induced sleep. Glancing at her phone as she grabbed it off the nightstand, she saw the time read two forty-five a.m. and tried to rub the sleep out of her eyes as she answered, not even taking note of the number on the screen.

"Hello?"

"Bug. Bug, you there?" The voice on the other end of the line was slurring but certainly familiar.

"King?" she asked groggily. "Do you know what time it is?"

"Shiiit, don't get me to lyin'," he laughed. "What you doing?"

She pulled the phone away from her ear, suddenly wide awake. Was this nigga serious? "Are you kidding me? It's almost three in the fucking morning, and you're asking me what I'm doing? You've lost your fucking mind." Making the move to hang up, she heard his voice come through the phone again.

"Bug, don't do me like that. Shit, a nigga can't just call to talk?"

"King, are you drunk?" He was really blowing her mind right now. What type of time was he on?

"Maybe. I might've had a drink or two...or five. Actually, according to this empty bottle of whiskey, I might've had more than that."

The longer this conversation carried on, the more irritated she became. "I really do not have time for this bullshit right now."

King kissed his teeth. "What you mean? I miss you, Bug. How is that bullshit? I was sitting here, and damn, all I can think about is how pretty you are. How good you used to look in that Oakwood Challengers jersey dress I got you that one year for Valentine's Day. How you looked even better when—"

"Uh-uh, absolutely not!" Lizzie said, sitting up and swinging her legs so that her feet were flat on the floor. She felt Alonzo stir beside her. "I am not doing this inappropriate ass walk down memory lane with you."

"Fuck you mean, inappropriate? Why, 'cause you got ole boy over there?"

"You mean my husband?" she hissed. "Yeah, absolutely. Not only that, it's the middle of the fucking night, and you're clearly looking for some attention that I cannot, will not, and do not want to give you. There ain't shit you should have to say to me at this time of night, especially not when you're drunk as hell, clearly in your feelings." As her voice started to rise, she felt the bed shift again, and this time, Alonzo's hand pressed against her back. She held up a finger before he could ask what was going on.

"Go to sleep, King. Hang up, sleep it off, or hell, call some-body else. Just don't pull this shit with me again because I promise you, I will not only block you from my phone, I will block you indefinitely from my life."

Lizzie didn't waste any more time waiting to hear his response. She simply hung up and tossed the phone down in its original place. As she turned to look at Alonzo, she could see that he was fuming.

"I swear, I'm about to lose my shit. I'm calling him first thing and cussing him out again because I'm sure he won't remember shit I just said to him."

He didn't answer her at first, choosing instead to place his hand on the back of her neck and pull her in as his lips pressed against her temple. "Nah, baby. I think it's time that King and I had a little chat. Man to man."

CHAPTER 19

Alonzo

Why the hell does this week feel stressful as hell?

That was the only question that was going through Alonzo's mind as Wednesday afternoon rolled around. Of course, he knew the answer to his question. There was, after all, a method to his madness. With their anniversary and party only three days away, Alonzo wanted to make sure he did everything possible to give the weekend his undivided attention. There was also the added element of the relaxing vacation he had planned for Lizzie for the following week that required getting some work done so he could be out of the office and stress-free. As a result, both he and Oliver had been pulling long nights the past couple of days. It'd been a miracle that he'd been able to make his date night with Lizzie on Monday if he was being honest.

"If you take a look at the numbers on page eleven of your report, you'll see that with your current strategy of splitting your investments between the current top earners and a few up-and-coming tech companies that show quite a bit of promise, we anticipate a significant increase in—"

Whatever Oliver was getting ready to say during his presentation with one of their newly acquired customers was cut off by Martha making her way into the conference room. His assistant rarely interrupted their meetings unless the situation was important or there was an emergency.

"I'm sorry, Mr. Langston, you have a visitor here. He says he's supposed to be meeting with you soon."

His eyes flicked toward the clock. 3:15 p.m. He wasn't expecting any visitors. This was their last meeting for the day, and afterward, he had planned to be locked in his office going over a few other client profiles for the rest of the afternoon.

Confused, he stood and followed Martha out into the hall. "Who is it?"

"I've never seen him before, but he said his name is King Holden? Tried to charm his way into seeing you and didn't take too kindly to me saying that you were occupied with a client and that he didn't seem to have an appointment. Quite frankly, he seems to take his name a bit too seriously if you don't mind me saying."

Ahh…of course. The other source of his stress this week. Alonzo supposed he should have expected a visit from King, especially after the message he'd left on the younger man's voicemail after his middle-of-the-night stunt, saying that they needed to talk. Still, it was pretty bold of him to just show up at Alonzo's office unannounced.

A chuckle escaped him. "No, I don't mind you saying at all. We should be finished up here soon, so escort him to my office and have him wait there." She nodded and headed off to do as he asked.

Walking back into the conference room, he apologized for the interruption and settled in for the rest of the meeting. While he made sure to focus, picking up and answering the questions that were more in his purview than his partner's, he tried not to get distracted by the confrontation he knew was coming. It was probably too much to hope that King would be apologetic about his behavior or willing to have a civilized conversation.

Oliver wasted no time asking what Martha wanted as soon as they'd finished with the clients and walked them to the elevator.

"King is here."

"Now, why the fuck would he be here? How does he even know how to find your ass?"

Alonzo shrugged. "I'm sure his presence has something to do with the message I left him after he pulled some disrespectful shit the other day. And as far as your second question, I mean, Oakwood is only so big. He knows what I do for a living, so all he really had to do was a quick web search, and it probably came right up."

As they came to a stop in front of his office door, Oliver looked skeptical. "Let me know if you need me," he said before heading toward his own office to give the two men some privacy.

Before walking in, Alonzo took a deep breath to steel himself against whatever was waiting for him on the other side of the door.

"King. Not the face I expected to see today, but it's good to see you." At least one out of two of those statements was true, so that had to count for something, right? Keeping his tone pleasant, Alonzo walked toward where he was sitting and offered his hand for a shake.

After standing and looking down at it, the expression on his face unimpressed, King returned the gesture. "Well, I mean, you called up my phone leaving messages and whatnot, so clearly you want to have a talk about something. I was in the neighborhood with some time on my hands, so I figured, why not drop in and see what it is you think we need to talk about."

Alonzo chose to ignore the attitude radiating from the other man, holding on to some sort of hope that this interaction could be a positive one. He also chose not to point out that in order to "be in the neighborhood," King had to go through the trouble of figuring out where Alonzo's office was located. That wasn't the point and would more than likely only add more fire to the flame.

"Understood, and I appreciate that. Things have been a bit busy with Lizzie and my anniversary coming up, so it's probably a good thing you decided to catch up with me because, yeah, we do need to talk."

"About?"

"About that phone call you made to my wife in the middle of the night the other day."

King shrugged. "What about it?"

So that's how he was going to play it?

"Listen, I understand that this shit is new for all of us, so it's going to take some getting used to. And I get why you might be tempted to reminisce when you see Lizzie like you did when you met her and Christian at the arcade or when you came over for dinner. Y'all have history, so that's to be expected. What's not expected is you calling my wife at almost three in the morning, being drunk and disrespectful. That crosses a line." Alonzo tried to keep his tone firm and hoped that none of the anger or hostility that he'd felt the other night came through. The last thing he wanted to do was escalate this situation, especially in his place of business.

Unfortunately, it didn't appear as though he and King were on the same page. "If you're feeling threatened, big dog, just say that."

"Threatened?" Alonzo scoffed.

"I mean, obviously, since you're trying to keep her on a short leash and whatnot. Making her tell you about our private conversations and shit."

Strike one.

"A short leash? Not at all. We just have a relationship and marriage built on mutual respect, communication, and honesty. And because of that, I know that she finds your behavior just as disrespectful as I do." Alonzo leaned down, placing his hands on top of the empty chair in front of him but in between the two of them.

"Yeah, aight. If that's the case, why didn't *she* make a move to tell me that?"

"She did," Alonzo said, his patience growing thin. "But considering you were letting the whiskey think and talk for you Monday night, you may not remember her making that clear. So, this is me doing it for her because as a husband, I know how to play my role."

King moved around the chair, closing the distance between them just a bit. Having him in his space didn't sit right with Alonzo, especially considering what was coming out his mouth right now, so he straightened but didn't back away.

"You keep throwing that marriage shit in my face like it's supposed to mean something to me. All I see is a nigga out here playing happy home with my family, and now that I'm back in the picture, ready to work shit out and whatnot, you're clearly starting to realize that your spot was temporary."

Strike two.

"Wooow." Alonzo couldn't help but laugh, which clearly struck a nerve with King. "That imagination of yours is just out here running wild, huh? The only thing you're out here working shit out about is a relationship with my son. And make no mistake, that shit is by the grace of me and Lizzie."

"Is that so?" The tension in the room grew tenfold as King tried to pull up to his full height.

"Absolutely. A true fact of the situation at hand. So, I'll say it again, all that late-night calling shit you seem to be on or what-ever romantic interest you think you have in my wife, I suggest you let go of it right now. The only thing you need to be worried about is building a relationship with Christian. Maybe put more of your energy into that and figure out what being a father entails."

"You know, it's real funny how you're out here trying to tell me how to move when it comes to my son. And I know you think you have some authority in this shit and whatnot because you put a lil' ring on Bug's finger, but the day I let another man dictate my relationship with my son is the day hell freezes over. If there's any discussion that needs to be had, it's that one."

Alonzo wanted nothing more than to wrap his hands around King's neck and squeeze. It was wild to think this man had the balls to sit up in his face, in his office, and insinuate that he had any right to dictate what went on in the Langston household. Instead of doing what he wanted to do, Alonzo took a step back. It appeared King took that as some sort of concession, his actions growing bolder.

"And as far as Bug is concerned, well, let's be honest, those few little years y'all are celebrating don't really have shit on the ten years that we have together. That's an actual milestone, and just one of many, if I have anything to say about it." Taking another step into Alonzo's personal space, he added, "And I damn sure intend on showing her just how much I missed her. It won't be hard at all to find out if that pussy still curves to my dick."

Strike muthafucking three.

Within seconds, Alonzo had the other man snatched up by his collar and, after three strides, slammed against the office wall. The force of it shook the framed pictures and degrees on the wall, each one threatening to fall, but Alonzo couldn't care less.

"What the fu—"

"I think you may be a bit confused about a few things, so let me clear it up for you," he said, his grip tight and unrelenting. "First, I am Christian's father. Me! And while I wholeheartedly support him getting to know you, trust and believe that replacing me in his life isn't even an option. I've been here, and I'm going to continue being here come hell or high water. And trust me, I'm both."

King struggled against his hold, but with the anger burning

through him, he wasn't going anywhere until Alonzo deemed it so. "Keeping you from him isn't what I want to do, but keep playing with me, and I promise you, you won't like the response from me nor Lizzie. Ask her and find out."

"Nigga, fuck you!" King spat, and Alonzo found himself chuckling again, unfazed.

"Now, as far as my wife is concerned, whatever you had with her is over and done with. You fucked that up and dropped that ball when you decided to abandon her in the hospital that day." Funny how King mentioned those ten years as if they gave him some sort of claim. Nevermind the fact that he'd been absent for the majority of them. Clearly the time he'd spent in the relationship didn't mean shit when it came to actually staying in Lizzie and Christian's life.

"You're right, three years is just a drop in the bucket, especially when you're talking about 'til death do us part. But make no mistake, I intend on celebrating the next fifty or sixty anniversaries with her for as long as God allows me to be on this earth and in her presence."

"Afraid of a little competition?" King hissed.

"Nah, but I am afraid about how I'm gonna explain to security and my staff why the fuck I had to break your jaw 'cause you couldn't stop disrespecting me or my wife. So, hear me when I say this because once I let you go, I expect you to scurry your ass out of my office." One of his hands let go of King's collar and gripped the man's jaw instead.

"When you see Lizette Noelle Langston, know that's me. Not because of that ring on her finger and not because I beat my chest and staked my claim on her like some fucking caveman. It's not even because I worship that piece of heaven between her legs every chance I get. It's because every day, she wakes up and chooses to love me just as much as I choose to love her. It's because she knows I'd sooner die behind her and Christian than see either one of them hurt. Every goddamn day we love, respect, and choose one another. Ain't shit you or anybody else can do to change that."

Alonzo released him, causing King to hit the floor before scrambling to his feet.

"The next time you make the mistake of forgetting that, I won't hesitate to break my foot off in your ass to make sure you remember."

After another moment, Alonzo took a few steps back and walked around to the other side of his desk. He took a seat, leaning back in his chair, and steepled his fingers, watching as King seemed torn between trying to come and beat his ass or running away with his tail between his legs.

"Now, it would be in your best interest to head home before I decide to stop being so nice and forget that I promised the woman I love that I wouldn't beat your ass. When we're ready for you to see *our* son again, we'll let you know. Until then, I suggest you play your role and get accustomed to getting to know Christian Langston on *our* terms. Martha will see you out. I have work to finish and a family to get home to."

CHAPTER 20

Lizzie

When Alonzo came home from work the night before and calmly recounted the events of his day, Lizzie had practically gone through the roof. She'd known that Alonzo had left a message with him saying he wanted to talk, and she'd known that King probably wouldn't receive that well. What she didn't expect, though, was for her baby daddy to show up at his place of business showing his ass. Mortified didn't even begin to cover how she felt. It'd taken the grace of God and Alonzo assuring her that he'd handled it to keep her from running out of the door and tracking his ass down so she could beat him twice over.

Unfortunately, she'd woken up that morning and found that a night of "cooling off" hadn't done a damn thing to improve her mood or feelings on the situation. So, while she should have been spending the day putting the finishing touches on her anniversary party, she'd spent the better part of her morning trying to track King's trifling ass down. He was ignoring her calls, but thankfully, after she'd called Morgan to explain the situation to her, she'd been more than happy to share his location with Lizzie on one condition: she wanted to be there when Lizzie confronted him. It took her a minute to agree, but once she did, she had what she needed to head over to King's new apartment.

"I swear I would pay a ridiculous amount of money to watch my brother-in-love hand that raggedy nigga his ass," Kendall snickered into the phone.

"It's not funny!" Lizzie said for the third time with an exasperated sigh. "King's ass was way out of pocket, Kay!"

"Oh, I completely agree, and honestly, no matter what he's going through, he had no right to pull that shit. I'm just saying, it's very rare to see Lonzo be anything but cool, calm, and collected, so I just know that was probably the show of the year."

Was her sister lying? No. Did that make her reaction any less aggravating? Again, no. She'd hoped, since Kendall typically tended to be a lot less rah-rah than Makayla, that talking to her would have helped level her out, but that hadn't happened either. It hadn't served any purpose other than giving Kendall a good laugh and irritating Lizzie even more.

That was perfectly fine, though, because she'd finally reached the apartment of the true object of her frustration. "Well, thank you for all of your non-help."

"You're welcome," Kendall quipped before wishing her luck and ending the call.

Once the line disconnected, Lizzie scanned the parking lot and spotted King's car in one of the reserved parking spots. She also spotted Morgan's car in one of the visitor spaces. After finding a parking space for herself, she took a deep breath.

"Here goes nothing," she whispered as she climbed out of the car. Closing her eyes and counting to ten, she hoped it would help focus her feelings. She knew everything about this situation was going to test both her patience and resolve, but it had to be done.

The two women met in the middle of the parking lot, and the pissed-off expression on Morgan's face made Lizzie pull up short.

"Okay, so before we go in there, I need to get something off of my chest."

Lizzie steeled herself for whatever was going to come next. "Listen, if you're about to sit up here and defend him, Morgan, you ca—"

"Oh, defending him is the last thing I came here to do. I plan on laying into him myself. Before we go upstairs, though, I just wanted to tell you that I'm so unbelievably sorry, Lizzie. Like you don't even understand."

"Why are you sorry? You're not the one who took your ass up to that office and showed out like a complete jackass," she laughed bitterly.

"Maybe not, but I am the person who got this ball rolling by giving him your number in the first place. I swear, every time I do something to help that boy get his life together, it turns around and bites me in the ass." Morgan shook her head.

"It's just lost on me what he thought he was going to accomplish by pulling that stunt."

"That's what I want to know."

"Well, I guess there's only one way to find out." Morgan nodded in agreement and led Lizzie up toward his apartment.

As they ascended the steps, Lizzie couldn't help but wonder how she would feel once she actually saw King. She didn't think she would bash his face in as soon as it was in front of her, but then again, at this point, anything was possible. Once they reached the door, Morgan began banging on it as though she were coming to collect rent or make an arrest. They only had to wait about thirty seconds before he opened it, and at the sight of him standing there in nothing but his basketball shorts with sleep in his eyes, Lizzie scrunched her nose in disgust. She'd bet money that they'd either just woken him up or interrupted him as he played some game.

"I hope you at least washed your ass today," Morgan said, pushing past him into his apartment. Lizzie followed suit. If she were here for any other reason, she might have been able to appreciate how nice his place appeared to be.

The surprise at both of them being there was clear on his face, but he did his best to try and hide it as he closed the door. "Of course, I did. What kind of man do you think I am, cuz?"

"I really don't think you want me to answer that question," she sneered.

That time, the surprise was clear as day and wasn't so easy to get rid of. "Well, damn. Tell me how you really feel."

"Oh, trust me, I intend to." No sooner than the words left her mouth did Morgan walk toward him and smack him clear upside his head. Lizzie couldn't hide her shock. Yeah, Morgan was clearly upset. This was a turn of events that she wasn't expecting.

"What the fuck was that for?"

"That was for you being an asshole." This time, she swung her purse at him, hitting him square in the chest. Even though he probably should have been, he hadn't expected that blow either. "And *that* was for putting me in the position to be utterly and completely embarrassed to have to call myself your cousin. I cannot believe you took your Black ass up to that man's place of business, acting like a full-grown child!"

"What are you talking about?"

"I'm talking about you thinking you were big and bold, going to see Alonzo, the man who has been raising your son, yesterday to call yourself trying to check him. Fuck choking you out, he should've flat-out beat your ass."

That comment clearly hit a nerve as King flushed red with shame.

"That's how you feel, Morgan? You're supposed to be my fucking family."

"And unfortunately, being related to you isn't something that I can change right now, though God knows I would if I could."

This time it was hurt that crossed his features. Instead of pointing that energy at the woman doing the swinging, he turned to Lizzie. "Yo, you talked to Morgan about this shit? First, you bring that nigga in our business, and now her?" He was clearly fuming and embarrassed, but if he knew what was good for him, he would direct that energy somewhere else.

"You brought other people into this when you decided to show your ass! Don't blame that on me because I can't take any of the credit."

Nodding in agreement, Morgan spoke up again. "Listen, you can settle whatever you need to with Lizzie in a minute, or better yet, she can light into your ass as much as she can and should, but first, you're going to hear what the fuck I have to say."

Lizzie moved a few steps back, taking a seat on the arm of the couch, giving herself a front-row seat for this interaction. Maybe Kendall was wrong about Alonzo and King being the show of the year; Morgan might take that award home.

"I swear to God, King, I'm so upset that I can barely see straight. Here I am going to bat for you, risking my friendship with Lizzie and my place in Christian's life to help you gain yours, and what do you do? You shit on my kindness and take advantage, just like you always do."

"Man, go ahead with all that noise," he said, kissing his teeth, clearly not trying to hear what she had to say. Lizzie's boundaries weren't the only ones that King didn't give a shit about.

"No, you go ahead with all that noise! You have done a lot of fucked-up shit in your life, King, including leaving your girlfriend and newborn child in the damn hospital and disappearing like a thief in the night, but I just…" The other woman let her words trail off.

"I've always made excuses for you. Even when you left, as horrible and painful as that was, I told myself over and over again that you'd make things right. That you'd come back once you realized what a big ass mistake you made. But here you are, bitching and moaning because the next man stepped up and did what you refused to do." She gave an exasperated laugh. "You know, at one point, I convinced myself that this was some weird case of cold feet. Some sort of reaction to the fact that you'd lost your parents and my parents, and that was why you were the way you were, but the truth is there's no one to blame but the man himself. I'm done trying to make what you do okay."

The pain behind her words made Lizzie stand and walk over to take her hand. There were genuine tears in the woman's eyes. Throughout their friendship, Lizzie had bitten her tongue because she knew how much King meant to Morgan. They'd settled into a truce over the years, agreeing not to talk about him with one another because as much shit as Morgan might let her talk, he was still her cousin. It seemed as if she'd finally reached her breaking point.

When it was clear that King had no response to her accusations, she wiped her face clean. "If our parents were here, they'd be just as ashamed of you as I am right now." Even Lizzie felt that punch to the gut.

"If all you're here to do is play some sick, twisted game, pack up your shit and go. Everyone, including Christian, will be a lot better off."

Turning to Lizzie, Morgan pulled her into a hug. After whispering another set of apologies in her ear, she pulled away. "I'll be outside if you need me. I'm done." Her gaze moved to King. "For real this time."

Without another word, Morgan walked out of the apartment, leaving King and Lizzie there staring after her.

CHAPTER 21

Lizzie

A piece of Lizzie felt bad about the conversation she needed to have. After getting his ass handed to him by Alonzo and Morgan back-to-back, she knew that King's ego was bruised beyond belief. And if this had been a few years ago, she might be content to leave things as they were, but she wasn't that person anymore. She didn't have the bandwidth to measure how much more he could take because, after all these years, it was time for her to have her say.

"Wow," King scoffed. "You really had my cousin in here wildin' out on me. And for what?"

I see this nigga really is hardheaded.

"I didn't have her in here doing anything. That's all you. And even if I did, what do you mean, *for what?* You're really going to sit here and ask me that? How about for how you called my phone at an ungodly hour, trying to reminisce and act like you wanted that old thing back? Or maybe because of the fact that you seem to think that just because I'm willing to let you get to know my son, you can say and do what you want after being gone for all of these years? And if that's not enough, maybe it would be for the way you showed up at my husband's job and got wildly disrespectful about him, my marriage, and apparently my pussy? Shit, if you want, we can go all the way back in time, and it can be for how it felt for you to abandon me not even two full days after I gave birth to Christian. Just tell me where you want me to start because, as you can see, I have plenty of material."

King sighed and rolled his eyes. "Straight into drama. I guess I should've figured that bitch ass man of yours would come running to tell you about our conversation. Ain't he a little old to have you fighting his battles?"

"First of all, stop with all the 'old' comments. It's not only an exaggeration but a tired one at that. Second of all, I don't need to fight his battles, especially not this one, since he already basically choked your ass out once." She shot him a pointed look.

"Third, you have this whole thing fucked up, King, because the reason why I'm here isn't his battle to fight. It's mine. Somewhere along the way over the last month, you seem to have gotten it into your head that you can do whatever the hell you want just because I've answered a few of your phone calls and let you see Christian a few times. That's not how this works!"

"Yeah, yeah, I hear all that noise, but I'm not about to sit up here and let that nigga dictate whether or not I can be around you or my son."

"Again, you've got it all the way wrong, so let me try this a different way. Get this through that thick ass skull of yours. You are not entitled to a *goddamn* thing. Not with Christian and certainly not with me. The only thing you need to be concerned about is trying to build a relationship with that beautiful little boy because that's what's important. Not you trying to get back whatever we had years ago. Not whatever made-up competition you have going on in your head with my husband. Not coming in here and trying to puff out your chest because you want to prove you're *that nigga*. It's childish as hell."

King took a step toward her, clearly pissed off about being

read the riot act. Despite his clenched fists, she knew he wasn't disrespectful enough to put his hands on her. He was a lot of things, but never that.

"You coming up in my place telling me about all the shit I'm doing wrong as if your nigga didn't put his hands on me. I hope you had this same energy for him."

As she turned away from him in disbelief, she threw her hands in the air. "And again, you're focused on the wrong shit! Why is it always everyone's fault except yours, King? You're talking real reckless right now as if you didn't start the whole mess."

"Because he's out here thinking he can take my spot!" he yelled out.

"There is no spot to take! YOU ARE NOT MY NIGGA! You haven't even met the bare minimum criteria to be a goddamn daddy. You are, quite frankly, none of the above right now."

King made a move to come closer, opening his mouth to interject, but Lizzie cut him off. "No, I'm not finished. I have plenty to say, and you're damn sure going to hear it. Don't ever presume that there will be a time when you can come in and tell me or Alonzo what you will and won't be doing. You don't run a damn thing around here except your mouth, as per usual. That's it, and that's all."

Lizzie's chest was heaving with the force of her anger. With each word, she felt like she was striking a blow that was owed to her for every time in her life when King had disregarded her, disrespected her, or simply disappointed her. Part of her had hoped that she could approach this situation with some sort of calm, but she was just so fucking mad.

Over the last couple of weeks, she'd convinced herself that maybe King showing up wasn't the disaster she initially imagined it would be. Was she still slightly uncomfortable? Yes, but if she was being honest with herself, that was partly because so many things had been left unsaid between them. She'd kept it bottled up, hoping the other shoe wouldn't drop and they could just move on. And if that honesty was going to go a bit further, that's part of why she was so angry now.

Now here she was, put into the very situation she'd been attempting to avoid, having to re-establish boundaries that King clearly didn't give a fuck about in the first place.

When it came down to it, she felt completely foolish for letting her guard down and letting King back into their lives. If this was his behavior after barely a month, what would it look like a few months from now? Would he even stick around that long, or was he only here to prove that he could claim what he thought was his?

"Why are you here, King?"

"What do you mean?"

"Exactly what I said. Why are you here? Why did you come back?"

He looked at her hesitantly, clearly unsure about whether or not she was going to start going off again.

"You know why I'm here."

Shaking her head, she took a seat on the arm of his couch. "No, actually, I don't. You said you wanted to get to know Christian, and sure, you've spent time with him, but it feels like you're more concerned about me and my relationship. So right here, right now, I'd really like to know why you came back."

Only silence followed her question. She wanted to give him time to process what she was asking, but she also wasn't interested in wasting her time. She said as much to him, fully prepared to leave, until he stopped her.

"Just…just give me a minute here, Bug. Talking feelings and shit has never been my strong suit. That still hasn't changed."

Lizzie nodded, even though the silence was making her feel antsy.

"No matter what, I'm still gonna be the nigga who left you

high and dry with a newborn baby. Let's be honest, you ain't trying to hear nothing I have to say about that situation."

"There you go, speaking for me again."

"I mean, I don't know what you want me to say. Yeah, we talked about having a family, but once I actually saw it, it became so…real. And suddenly, I just didn't know what to do. I never intended to leave you at the hospital, but I got home, and I just… panicked."

"So your solution was to just leave altogether?" she asked incredulously.

He at least had the decency to look embarrassed by his admission. Rubbing the back of his neck, he said, "I figured you had your mom, your sisters, friends. People that could help you with whatever you needed."

"But Christian wasn't their responsibility, King! None of them laid down and helped me get pregnant. None of them begged me to keep the baby so they could 'finally have a real family.' Isn't that what you said to me?"

"Yeah, but I was scared, Bug!"

"And so was I! Scared with a newborn and a boyfriend who wanted nothing to do with us and didn't even have the decency to say anything before he left!"

Before she started yelling again, she took a deep breath and counted to ten like she'd done before she arrived. "Again, why did you come back?"

Leaning against the wall, his hands went to his pockets, but his eyes never left her. "Morgan's been telling me for years to come home, that I have family here, look at what I've been missing out on. I guess I just got tired of hearing that shit and finally decided to listen. Having to hear over and over again that a nigga took your spot? That shit messes with you."

She wasn't sure what sort of reaction he was expecting from her. She could understand being afraid of the unknown, but that didn't excuse what he'd done. He could have come back at any time, and he chose not to. After saying those words aloud, the silence set in again.

"I'm not going to apologize for moving on with my life, King. And things are not going back to how they were all those years ago. It's unrealistic, and if that's what you're expecting, you're going to be extremely disappointed."

"All I want is a chance."

"But see, it's clear we have a difference of opinion on what that chance should be. I'm not interested in anything from you other than trying to get to know Christian, and honestly, you're on thin ice with that."

She stood and made her way toward the door. "I think, for now, it's best that we take time to calm down and figure out where to go from here. You need to decide whether or not you can accept the way things are in my life. Getting to know Christian and building a relationship with him means respecting the boundaries that I set and accepting the role that Alonzo has in both of our lives."

The sounds of King kissing his teeth and mumbling under his breath let her know he was still on the same bullshit. "I'm serious, King. You need to figure your shit out. Alonzo is my husband and Christian's father. If you can't come to terms with that, then maybe you should do what Morgan said and do us all a favor by leaving."

She opened the door and made a move to leave before stopping to turn and look at him. "Christian wants to know you. If you can be the person you claim you want to be, then I want him to know you. But I won't facilitate that at the cost of my peace, my family, or my happiness."

With those final words, she made her way downstairs to her car. Morgan was there, ready to pull her into a hug. After promising to see each other on Saturday at the party, they went their separate ways. As she made her way home, Lizzie could admit that she felt like a weight had been lifted from her shoulders. No matter what King decided to do, she'd said her piece and gotten what she needed to off of her chest. Whatever decision he decided to make, it wouldn't be her burden to hang onto. And even if he decided sticking around wasn't what he was going to do, she knew that she and Alonzo would pick up the pieces and make sure that Christian was okay because, as his parents, that's what they were built to do.

CHAPTER 22

Alonzo

"Mmmm, baby, we're going to be late."

"I don't think it's possible to be late to our own party, princess. We're the guests of honor."

"T-T-That's exactly what I'm s-s-saying."

Alonzo found himself smiling against the inside of her thigh at the way her voice caught when he nibbled on her.

She was right. They were supposed to be getting dressed so they could get to the party, which was set to start in…twenty minutes? Thirty? Honestly, he wasn't sure. He'd lost track of both the time and task at hand when Lizzie came strutting out of the bathroom, fresh out the shower, wrapped in a towel that had just been begging to be snatched away.

He'd managed to get it off her, pull her into the bed, and convince her to use his face like her favorite chair so quickly that, if you asked him, he deserved a medal. Thank goodness they'd dropped Christian off with Kendall and Greg earlier in the day. They would be bringing him to the party, and then he'd go back home with them to get some time with his cousins.

"*Fuuuuck.*"

Lizzie's whines were music to his ears. It wasn't difficult to know that Alonzo was well on his way to sending her into her second orgasm. The way her thighs gripped either side of his head and her juices ran down his beard as she rode his face to paradise and back told him everything he needed to know. His hand collided with her ass, causing her hips to lose their rhythm. He wished he could see the way her hands were gripping the headboard, but right now, he was focused on wrapping his lips around her clit while his tongue played with it like an expert musician.

He groaned as her thighs began to shake. Ready to push her over the edge, Alonzo allowed his tongue to slip away from her hardened bud and slide down further until it swirled against her other entrance. The gasp she let loose only encouraged him as he made a mess of her. Once it was just as slick as her pussy lips, he shifted back to her clit, allowing one, then two fingers to take its place, sliding easily into her ass. His fingers fucked in and out of her, setting a punishing pace. He got exactly what he wanted as her screams echoed through the bedroom and she gushed all over his face just the way he liked.

She took advantage of his loosened grip and slid down his body with shaky legs, a fire sparked inside of her if the look on her face was any indication. "You ready to slide down on that dick, princess?"

"Not quite."

He immediately knew he was in for some shit, even before she found herself eye-to-eye with his hardened dick. Her tongue took a swipe at the precum that had pooled at his tip, and she moaned like it was the best thing she'd ever tasted.

"You gonna play with it or take care of it?" he growled.

The way she giggled in response only seemed to make him harder. They both knew how much he loved it when she teased him until he couldn't take it anymore. The taste of her on his tongue had him ready to bust right on its own, so it was no surprise when he buried his fingers into her short hair and pushed against her lips.

She opened immediately, the vibrations from her moans shooting straight to his balls. He felt borderline obsessed with the feel of her tongue lapping at the underside of his dick as she bobbed up and down enthusiastically, taking as much of him into her mouth as she could. When she gagged at the feel of Alonzo hitting the back of her throat, he groaned, his toes curling and eyes fluttering. A sharp pain hit him in the thigh, and he looked down to see her nails digging in. He chuckled because she loved having his eyes on him just as much as he loved watching her.

"Don't worry, princess. No way I'd miss a second of—*shit!*" That last word came out as a grunt because what else was he supposed to do when she was relaxing her throat to take all of him repeatedly while watching him with those big, watering eyes? His hips thrust upward, and she did nothing but hold on tight to him, letting him set the pace.

As much as he wanted to finish down her pretty little throat, he wanted to slide into her pussy even more. He made quick work of pulling her off his dick, pleased with himself as she gasped for air.

"Show me how well you ride this dick." It was a command, not a suggestion, and it must have been just what she had in mind if the way she scrambled up and positioned herself over him was any indication.

They let out matching groans as her warmth engulfed him, and his beautiful wife wasted no time sliding back up and then impaling herself onto him again and again.

"*Soooo* good," she whined, her hands pulling at her own strands as her hips swirled after every lift.

Alonzo watched in awe as she took his length over and over again. It never ceased to amaze him how gorgeous she looked in moments like these, skin glistening and jaw slack as she chased her own pleasure while giving him his.

"Mmm…how good?"

She only moaned in response, her hands planting themselves on his chest as she ground down on his dick, fucking him as if her life depended on it.

"Must be damn good," he grunted with an upward thrust that caused a gasp to leave her lips. "Because you're making a fucking mess all over my lap." That led to a whimper as she went harder, now trying to keep up with the strokes he was giving her from underneath. "Not even ashamed, are you, princess?" He leaned up, arm capturing her waist and pulling her chest tight to his. "No, I think you love drenching my dick like this. Leaving it soaking wet so that you can clean it up afterward." He felt her pussy clench at his words, getting even wetter than what should be possible at this point.

"What are you waiting for?" He tightened his grip as he hit her with upward strokes. Her head fell back, giving him perfect access to her neck. He wasted no time attacking it, the strokes of his tongue matching the way he was fucking her, his teeth scraping her skin as the sounds leaving her lips grew in volume. It wasn't until he felt her walls tighten with another orgasm that he finally let go of his own, growling into her neck as he fucked his release into her again and again and again. And just as he'd predicted, when it was all said and done, his loving wife cleaned up the mess they'd made without an ounce of hesitation.

CHAPTER 23

Lizzie

"Explain to me how you're late for your own anniversary party," hissed Kendall, lightly snatching Lizzie up by her elbow.

"Well, I would, big sis, but I don't think you actually want those types of details about my sex life."

Kendall's response of "Gross!" came at the exact same time as Makayla's mischievous grin and comment that Lizzie was "definitely a woman after my own heart."

Despite her initial half-assed protests, the sex that she'd just been given was exactly what she needed to start the night off. Quite frankly, if she hadn't been looking forward to this party for so long, she'd be face down, ass up as her husband slid right back into her, ready and waiting for her next orgasm. For now, though, she'd save that for the end of the night when they made it back home. In the meantime, she had a party to enjoy.

The whole vibe in Midnight Trail was just what she'd hoped for. The beer and whiskey seemed to be flowing, based on the level of laughter in the room, and most of their guests were gathered on the dance floor as "Anniversary" by Tony! Toni! Toné played through the speakers to signify their arrival. Everyone looked amazing in their cowboy boots, jackets with fringes, and plaid and button-up shirts. It was definitely the Black cowboy affair that she wanted. As her eyes perused the food set up, she knew she would need to grab a few ribs and soon if the way Percy and Oliver were battling over who could load the most up onto their plate was any indication of how good they were.

Everyone they loved was present, including some of her closest clients, the stylists from her shop, and Alonzo's employees from the firm. It looked as though they were all ready to party well into the night.

"Mommy!"

Christian and his cousins appeared in front of her, seemingly out of thin air. He looked even more adorable than she'd imagined in his little boots and black cowboy hat that matched the one Alonzo wore.

"We're going to take pictures on the horse!"

"Horse?" Lizzie said, turning to Alonzo in alarm. She knew she came up with this theme and all, but she damn sure didn't remember signing off on a horse.

"It's a prop, princess. Relax," he chuckled. "Dana told me that they found an antique rocking horse. It hadn't been delivered when we came last time, but it just arrived yesterday, if I'm not mistaken. She'd already been looking for one to go with the regular decor, but I think she was excited to put it out tonight because it went so well with the theme."

Lizzie took a breath, happy that she wasn't going to have to curse anyone out over a live animal.

"Can I have everyone's attention?"

They both turned as Makayla's voice came over the microphone. Her sister was on stage, a bright smile on her face and affection in her eyes. "Now that the guests of honor have *finally* arrived," she shot them a knowing look, and the guests laughed, having guessed why they were probably late, "we can officially get this thing started. Y'all are probably all well aware of who I am, but just in case, I'm Lizzie's big sister, Makayla." She took a small bow, which drew more laughter from the crowd.

"I don't think there's anyone on this earth that could love my baby sister the way she deserves to be loved other than Alonzo Langston. I mean, who else is going to indulge her love of country music to the point where he let her plan this entire party around it?"

Lizzie rolled her eyes at that statement. They were seriously going to have to stop clowning her about this.

"Anyway, baby sis, questionable taste aside, these last three years, we've all watched you, Lonzo, and Christian grow into a family like no other. Thank you for allowing all of us to not only bask in your love in all its glory but also be active players in your story, not just tonight but every day since you've met." Lizzie's eyes began to glaze over with tears, and she felt Alonzo tuck her into his side as he kissed the top of her head.

"So, everybody, eat up, throw those drinks back, and let's spend the night celebrating the fact that these two beautiful people have truly found forever in one another."

Her mother appeared on stage, two shot glasses in hand, and the two of them clinked the glasses before throwing them back, leading the collective as everyone in the room who had a drink did the same.

"And also, y'all might wanna go ahead and get drunk because Lizzie has requested that each and every person here engage in an obscene amount of line dancing throughout the night."

"You're damn right!" Lizzie yelled.

With those last few words, the deejay dropped the next song, this time "Throw It Back" by BRELAND and Keith Urban. Right on time, Raven showed up next to her with a shot of what she guessed was Uncle Nearest for her to throw back, just like the song instructed. She gladly took it and did just that before grabbing her best friend's hand and heading to the dance floor to throw something else back.

The next couple of hours were filled with nothing but laughter, good food, and great company. Despite all the grumbling they'd done, her sisters ended up doing more line dancing than she did, especially once Dana and Malcolm joined in on the fun and showed their guests just how it was done.

Now, as she swayed back and forth in Alonzo's arms, her back pressed to his front with his face nuzzled right next to her ear, she couldn't feel anything but happiness. The love that filled this room doubled in size as she listened to him sing along with Kane Brown's "Worship You." Was this man secretly trying to sing the drawers off of her right in the middle of the dance floor? If so, it was working.

As the song came to a close, he whispered, "I forgot to mention something."

"And what would that be?"

"I got a call earlier today. From King."

That was a shock. They hadn't talked about King since she'd come home after meeting with him on Thursday and told Alonzo what happened, nor had she heard from King himself. There was no use in focusing on him when they had so many other things happening and so they'd agreed to put him on the back burner and focus on celebrating their love. In light of that and what had happened the last time the two men had spoken, she was shocked to hear that they'd been in contact.

"What did he say?"

"Not much. We weren't on the phone for long. He mentioned wanting to meet up to talk, and I told him that once there was some free time in my schedule, I'd let him know."

Lizzie turned in his arms so that she could see his face. "Should we be worried, or do you thi—"

Alonzo cut her off, pressing a soft kiss to her lips. "I think we won't know what he's going to do until we have that conversation. I'm willing to sit down with him, and as long as he doesn't have a problem, neither do I. But we're not going to worry about that right now because you and Christian have me, no matter what."

His words brought a smile to her face, but he clearly wasn't done. "Besides, we won't know for a while because I'm all booked up for the next week."

This time Lizzie tilted her head in confusion. "Doing what?"

"Because we have an anniversary trip to go on. The first of two."

"Oh my God!" Lizzie screamed. Heads turned in their direction, drawn by the outburst.

"I thought you were going to get down on one knee when you gave her the ring, Lonzo! That don't look like one knee to me."

Lizzie turned toward Oliver, who wasn't standing too far from the couple. "Ring?"

The other man mumbled something that sounded suspiciously like "oops" as Alonzo let out a groan. "Thanks for that, man," he said with a chuckle while shaking his head. "Well, since the cat's already out of the bag…"

His sentence trailed off as he got down on one knee, sending Lizzie's feelings into a tailspin. Her eyes watered, and the tears flowed freely as she gazed down at one of the most important people in her life. They started falling even faster as Christian walked over, a shy expression on his face and a small box in his hands. He handed it to Alonzo, who pulled him in closer. "Your two favorite men decided that you deserve the world. We can't fit the world in this box, princess, but what we could fit in it was this." He whispered something to Christian, who nodded and helped him open the box to reveal the most beautiful ring settings she'd ever seen. Her original wedding set was gorgeous, but as the rings in the box caught the light, she had to admit there was no comparison.

"What do you think, mommy?" Christian said, clearly excited.

She smiled. "I think...that it's beautiful, baby. I love it."

The entire room cheered as Alonzo stood and replaced her current set with the new one. Lizzie lifted Christian in her arms and peppered him with kisses until he couldn't stop giggling and begged her to stop. After finally setting him down so that he could go find his cousins, she turned to her husband.

As she stood on her toes to place a kiss on his lips, she hoped it conveyed every emotion she was feeling. The joy, the love, the attraction, and the beauty. "You know," she said when they finally separated, "as beautiful as this is, I hope you don't plan on giving me a new ring every few years. I'll never be able to top that."

"Princess, we have the rest of forever together, and I'm going to spend every second spoiling you one way or another. Besides, I have plenty of other ideas."

With a laugh, she gave him another quick kiss. "I love you," she whispered against his lips.

"Nowhere near as much as I love you."

Epilogue

ALONZO

"Have I mentioned lately how much I love your husband?" Makayla asked as the three sisters stood at the bar, waiting for their drinks.

Alonzo smirked at the praise. "I love you, too, sis," he called out from his position in the private cabana the group had rented.

"Not too much now," Lizzie scolded. "You have your own man, remember? That one belongs to me."

"Yeah, yeah, yeah, but I'm just saying. How many brothers-in-law would gift their wife with an all-expenses-paid anniversary trip to the Maldives, complete with her sisters and their men? Don't worry, I'll wait."

Alonzo couldn't help the chuckle that escaped him.

"Probably not many," Lizzie said with a shrug, "but that's why I love him. We had our private vacation, but he knew how much spending time with y'all has meant to me lately, so he made it happen."

The wink that she sent his way was one he returned. The truth was Lizzie had been saying for months that now that she and her sisters were back on track with their relationship, she wanted to take at least one of their girls' nights international. The two of them had also been talking at length about wanting to visit the beautiful island for quite a while, so for him, combining the two for a weeklong trip just seemed like the perfect thing to do.

Each couple had their own private overwater bungalow, connected by a small boardwalk, which also connected to the main areas of the adults-only resort. The March weather was perfect, and he had to admit that he was glad he'd chosen to schedule the trip a month and a half after their anniversary. Watching his gorgeous wife prance around in a muted brown bikini that complimented her skin perfectly was even more confirmation they'd made the right choice.

She was glowing and looked like she didn't have a care in the world as she teased Kendall about not being able to handle whatever fruity drink she'd ordered. Checking the lounge chair next to him, Reggie looked just as content as he was. He'd thought he would have to strong-arm the other man into allowing him to cover the entire trip, but Reggie only asked for the details, stated he would cover anything the older man needed him to, and made sure to emphasize that he'd return the favor before the year was out. With the way he traveled, Alonzo had no doubt he'd be getting him back on some level very soon.

It was inevitable that his thoughts eventually drifted toward Greg. With the issues that he and Kendall seemed to be going through, no one had been sure if the couple would agree to come. Thankfully, they had, but Greg's involvement in the trip so far hadn't been the greatest. In the three days they'd been there so far, he'd gone on an excursion with them and joined them for meals, but during times like these, when they were just relaxing taking time at the pool or on the beach, he made himself scarce.

Alonzo knew how much Greg loved his wife, but the man was blowing it. This was the perfect opportunity for them to reconnect, and instead, he seemed to be wasting it. He made a mental note to grab Reggie and insist on a boy's night out tonight while their partners took their dedicated time together. Maybe they could talk some sense into him. If not, Alonzo wasn't sure what would become of their marriage.

"Penny for your thoughts."

The feel of his wife climbing into his lap was enough to set him on edge and force him to suppress a groan. You'd think he hadn't been buried deep inside of her just a few hours ago.

"Just wondering how I got so lucky," he answered, not wanting to spoil the mood.

"Fate," she responded confidently. She wasn't wrong. "I wish the time difference wasn't so spread out here. I want to call and talk to Christian."

"Don't pout," Alonzo found himself saying. "You know I can't resist you when you pout." He placed a kiss on her lips for good measure. "You can call and talk to him after we have dinner later. I'm sure he'll be up by then and ready to tell you all about his weekend with King."

Reaching a good place with the other man hadn't been easy, but they'd been doing their best to make things work. After returning from their first anniversary trip, Alonzo had a sit-down with King that, unfortunately, didn't end well at all. Things didn't get physical, which was certainly an improvement, but the two did exchange some pretty heated words. It took another two weeks before they were able to meet again.

That meeting certainly went better than the first two, but things were far from perfect. The important thing was they'd seemed to reach a bit of common ground on the disrespect, though Alonzo wasn't sure if King would ever fully stop trying to challenge him in little ways. His relationship with Christian seemed to be thriving, which was what everyone wanted.

While Delilah was keeping all of the grandkids for the week, Alonzo and Lizzie had agreed to let Christian spend Saturday night to Sunday with King for their second-ever sleepover. He knew Lizzie was worried about it, but Morgan was keeping an eye on things and had Raven, Delilah, and Percy on speed dial if necessary.

"I know, I just miss him," she sighed.

"Well, how about we do something to take your mind off of that?" His fingers grazed the side of her suit bottoms, ready to make their way underneath the flimsy fabric.

"Aht, aht!" Kendall said, coming over and grabbing for Lizzie before he could go any further. "If we let y'all get started now, we'll never get her back."

The group laughed as Lizzie stood. "Party pooper."

"Don't worry, baby, she can't hide you from me forever."

"Not at all," she said, sending a smile his way that hit him straight in the heart. He couldn't wait to get her alone later. If they were lucky, they might not even make it to dinner tonight. A man could dream.

A Final Word

If you read my debut, Worth It, then you were already slightly familiar with Alonzo and Lizzie. Originally, I didn't think there was a story for them, but obviously they proved me wrong. As long as I've been writing (and I've been writing a long time, even before I decided to publish), I've never attempted an established couple before so I hope that I did them a bit of justice.

I hope you not only enjoyed this story, but that you're also able to find the time to leave a rating and/or review on your favorite platform (Amazon, Goodreads, Storygraph, etc.) They're the best way to help readers find new favorites and are so important in terms of indie author support.

To keep up-to-date on upcoming Lady Marie projects, be sure to sign up for the Spice In Your Life Newsletter, join me on Patreon (Lady Marie Affair), check out my linktree, and follow me on social media @ladymariewrites.

To order a signed copy of any of my physical projects, merch, or web exclusives, please visit the Lady Marie Shop at lady mariewrites.com

Acknowledgments

My beta readers are everything. I'm not exaggerating when I say they were instrumental in flushing out these characters and bringing them to life. To Jaleesa, Paris, Lynell, and Kai, thank you ten times over for sticking with me through this journey and bringing out the best in not only me, but also Alonzo and Lizzie. And thank you for pushing through those ARC reads to see just what your hard work and critique brought to fruition.

To Ty and Mychele, thank you both for loving Reggie and Makayla enough to take a chance on Alonzo and Lizzie's ARC. Your love and support mean the world to me.

To Big Tanon, no way could I forget you! You put up with my mess through ARC reading, promo help, and all my regular degular shenanigans time and time again. And while we're here, Big Shon, too. I love both of y'all for being my peer sounding boards and never getting tired of me. I'm keeping you both. You've been warned.

And to my sissa because you've always known I've had this in me. Thank you for pushing me to include therapy in Lizzie's book and knowing that it was just what this story, and Black women in general, need no matter what the world tells us. I love you!

And of course to my readers, whether old or new, thank you for taking this ride with me. I hope you're buckled up because I've got quite a few more in me and I'm taking each and every one of y'all along.

Also by Lady Marie

SISTERS & SERENDIPITY SERIES

Worth It (A Fake Dating Novel)

Found Forever (An Established Couple, After the HEA Novella)

SUGARED AND SPICED SERIES

Sugar, Sugar (An Age Gap, Sugar Arrangement Novella)

Sweet Heat (A FFM Age Gap, Sugar Arrangement Novella)

Sugar-Coated Kisses (An Age Gap Insta-love Novella)

Sweet Control (An Age Gap, Sugar Arrangement Novella)

SLEIGH THE NIGHT COLLECTION

After Tonight (A Brother's Best Friend Novella, *Sleigh the Night* Prequel)

Sleigh the Night (A Winter Shorts Collection)

HOLIDAY NOVELLAS AND SHORT STORIES

With Sugar on Top (A Sugared and Spiced NYE Short)

Sinnamon & Golds (A Lick Back Season, Thanksgiving Novella)

Szn's Greetings (A Sinnamon & Golds Christmas Short)

Resolutions (A New Year's Novellette)